Ruth Sas

About the Author

ELLE EGGELS was born and raised in a small town in the
southern Netherlands. A fashion journalist, she gave up her
career to travel and begin writing, settling in San Cristóbal de las
Casas in Chiapas, Mexico. She now lives in Holland.

The House of the
Seven Sisters

The House of the
Seven Sisters

A Novel of Food and Family

ELLE EGGELS

*translated from the Dutch
by David Colmer*

Perennial
An Imprint of HarperCollinsPublishers

First published in 1998 as *Het huis van de zeven zusters* by Uitgeverij Vassallucci, Amsterdam. This translation first published in 2001 by Picador, an imprint of Macmillan Publishers Ltd, London.

The first U.S. edition of this book was published in 2002 by William Morrow, an imprint of HarperCollins Publishers.

HarperCollins books may be purchased for educational, business, or sales promotional use. For information please write: Special Markets Department, HarperCollins Publishers Inc., 10 East 53rd Street, New York, NY 10022.

First Perennial edition published 2003.

Library of Congress Cataloging-in-Publication Data is available.

ISBN 0-06-056575-6

03 04 05 06 07 RRD 10 9 8 7 6 5 4 3 2 1

for Al

Now as they went on their way, he entered a village; and a woman named Martha received him into her house. And she had a sister called Mary, who sat at the Lord's feet and listened to his teaching. But Martha was distracted with much serving; and she went to him and said, 'Lord, do you not care that my sister has left me to serve alone? Tell her then to help me.' But the Lord answered her, 'Martha, Martha, you are anxious and troubled about many things; one thing is needful.'

LUKE 10:38–42

One

I didn't get to know my father until after his death. We were sitting in the courtyard. The heat was hanging over our table like a drunk who won't go away, and we were sipping grenadine we had chilled in the cellar, because this was back in the days before there was a fridge in every home – people still had big families, and kitchens were places with huge coal-burning stoves and long tables with lots of chairs.

It was one of those summer evenings when you can already feel the autumn nibbling away the daylight, and my aunts were telling stories about people I had never met. I couldn't put faces to any of the names, and that was why I didn't understand why the women kept on bursting into shrieks of laughter and doubling up over their knitting while the stitches slipped from their needles. Christina's laughter bounced through her wool for minutes at a time. She never actually managed to tell one of those weird and wonderful stories herself because the memories tripped her up before she could find the words to string them together – they stuck in her throat and almost choked her. Tears of laughter would roll down her round cheeks and, even though we never got to hear the story, we would gasp along with her until our stomachs felt like they had been put through a wringer and our insides ached from crotch to navel.

We had closed the bakery early that day after selling out of bread – the journeyman baker had gone swimming in the river and we couldn't do a second round of baking without him. It always amazed me how persistently people could knock on our doors and windows, even when they knew there weren't any tarts or loaves of bread left and that they would have to end up coming back the next day whether we answered or not.

But whoever was standing out there this time started hitting the shop window with a stick. The glass cried out and our laughter took cover in the cherry tree. The sisters wiped their cheeks and exchanged silent glances, looking from one to the other, knowing that it had to be something horrible out there on the pavement. In the end it was Camilla who slid back her chair and went to have a look. When she came back she spoke in a hushed voice and gave that horrible thing a name: 'Sebastian.' Then she covered her eyes and stood there frozen to the spot for hours to avoid seeing what had happened.

We walked into the hall in time to see two strangers carry a lifeless body into the living room and lay it down on the table. The man's jacket and trousers were torn to shreds, and the tattered edges were stiff with blood soaked up from his wounds. Someone had wrapped a blue-checked tea towel around his head and that was soaked with blood too. I was bundled back into the hallway. A little later the nun who was our district nurse showed up and hugged each of the women in turn. Then she looked at me and said, 'Poor child.' I took a quick step backwards before she had a chance to pull me into the range of her overpowering body odour as well. Christina told me to go out into the courtyard and wait with Oma. Through the cracked panes in the back door, I watched the women running back and forth with towels and basins of steaming water while their aprons swished over the wainscoting. It was like a scene from a silent movie.

'Oma,' I asked, 'who is that man?'

Without letting her knitting needles falter in the rhythm of their monotonous song, Oma mumbled that she had already knitted seven socks this week, even though her sweaty fingers had made the wool wet and lumpy.

Oma only ever knitted one kind of sock, but she never counted them in pairs, always as separate items. Whenever she finished a sock she just threw it into a basket with all the others. It was up to whoever needed new socks to sort through them in search of a pair – the socks all had the same number of stitches, but no two were ever exactly alike.

Oma paid no heed to the men who had turned up with the battered body. She didn't even seem to have noticed the sudden uproar in the house. Until she suddenly started talking in her strong German accent.

'Your papa, he was a beautiful man. He looked like that Roy Rogers. Your papa, he could have been in the movies. He played very nice, and horses he could ride too.'

The man everyone had been keeping quiet about for thirteen years was in there lying on our living room table, and I was supposed to stay outside?

The sun withdrew behind the bakery and took the light with it. Dinner never came and I stayed there waiting in the remnants of the evening with Oma. Finally Vincentia came out to get me. She buried her hands deep in her pockets – Vincentia was the first woman in the village to wear trousers – and said, 'You mustn't cry, you never even knew him.' Then she led me into the living room, which now smelt even worse than the fat nun's armpits. The table had been covered with a clean sheet that went all the way down to the floor. The laundry soap in the sheet tried to smother the smell of the corpse, and the musty brand-new pyjamas hugged the stiff body with embarrassed reluctance. A thin pillow had been slipped under the man's battered skull, and one hand had been draped over the other to hide his missing fingers. His hands might not have been clasped in prayer, but the nun had still managed to weave a rosary around those fingers of glass. The small crucifix with copper corpus was resting on his stomach, on top of the beige-and-tan-striped pyjamas. The dead man's bruised and battered cheeks were all puffed up and lumpy, as if his mouth were full of gobstoppers. There was a spotless plaster on his forehead, and a dark cloth had been tied around his head the way farmers wear them in summer to protect themselves from the sun.

Martha came the next day. We had just sat down to eat.

'Why did they bring him here?' she asked, pulling up a chair.

'They didn't know where else to take him,' answered Christina. 'He didn't have an address on him, and someone remembered him from here.'

'It's so long ago,' said Martha.

'He's still family,' whispered Marie, who was trying to manoeuvre a fish bone to the front of her mouth. Marie had been given permission to leave the convent for the funeral and had arrived that same day. 'He's still Emma's father,' she said.

'He's no family of mine any more,' Martha insisted.

I looked at her and wondered whether our family tie had lapsed now as well. It had been three years since we'd seen each other and she hadn't even said hello.

'Does he look very bad?' she asked.

'Don't worry. Sister Cyrilla laid him out beautifully,' said Clara.

After lunch Martha shuffled into the living room. I sat down on the staircase to wait for her to come back out again. I had so many questions to ask about the man who was laid out on the table we only ever used for special occasions. I was hoping Martha might answer them, but she stayed in the room all afternoon. Her sisters took turns to come and peek through a chink in the door before walking away again shaking their heads.

That evening I was told to take a bath after dinner, even though Wednesday was my usual bath day. Soft from the warm water and rubbed red with the coarse towel, I was given one of Camilla's dark dresses to wear. It fitted me almost perfectly – my aunt's figure was hardly any fuller than mine, even though she was a woman and I still had to become one. Soon the gap of twelve years in our ages wouldn't be enough to show where we stood in the family and Camilla had become increasingly uncertain as to whether she should mother me or treat me like a sister. We had been waiting for an event to mark my coming of age. My first period would have been the obvious choice, but I was late. Most of the girls at school had already stained their underpants and been excused from gym more than once. Whenever I asked Christina about it, she just brushed aside my questions by saying things like, 'You'll have to bear that cross long enough as it is.'

Sebastian's death took the place of the first signs of womanhood. The long-awaited blood came the day after the funeral, and after that I began wearing my aunts' clothes more and more often, until they gradually replaced all of the girl's dresses in the big wardrobe on the upstairs landing.

I felt funny in a grown-up's dress. As Christina steered me to the living room my stomach contracted. Half-digested food crept up my oesophagus and the taste of spinach and hard-boiled egg seared the back of my throat.

'Martha wants you to sit with him tonight,' said Christina.

Suddenly my dinner had no more desire to pursue the natural route – instead it was in a big rush to take the nearest short cut out of my body. I squeezed my throat shut, swallowed it all a second time and felt disgusted.

I hadn't been back in the foul-smelling living room since Vincentia had shown me the man in the striped pyjamas.

'We'll do it together,' said Christina. She smiled encouragingly while I clenched my teeth to hold back the rotten egg.

Seven candles on the sideboard in front of the statue of Our Lady of Lourdes threw a parade of flickering, prancing shadows onto the wall. Christina and I sat down on opposite sides of the table. My skin crawled. Unable to face the dead man or the monstrous procession on the wall, I looked down at my lap instead. We said three Rosaries and one Litany of the Saints. Then we sat quietly for a while, but the combination of motionlessness and silence was too much for me.

I closed my eyes, raised my head slowly, waited an eternity, then reopened my eyes. The dead man looked as if a pig's bladder had been pulled over his skull, and the corners of the plaster on his forehead were lifting. I searched for some sign of warmth in that face, but it just kept on staring up at the ceiling with an indifference that left ice flowers on my heart.

'He doesn't look a bit like Roy Rogers. Oma said he was handsome,' I whispered.

'The horses trampled him to death. He always looked good,' said Christina.

'Was he nice too? What did people like about him?' I asked, looking back at that frozen mask.

'He was fun, he was good for a laugh. And he had a really beautiful singing voice.'

'Did he love Martha?'

There was a moment's silence. 'I think so,' said Christina after a while.

'So why'd he leave?' I asked.

Christina shrugged. 'Maybe he wanted to love us all. It was too much. You can't love seven women at once.'

'Eight!'

'What?'

'Eight. I was there too, don't forget.'

Christina laughed, but not with her normal, cheerful laugh. 'He never got a chance to start loving you.'

Two

When Sebastian came into the seven sisters' lives, Martha was twenty-seven and he was yet to turn twenty-two. He was the new organist at the parish church. Anne and Christina brought him home with them after a rehearsal of the girls' choir, and after that first time he just kept on coming. He started off as a regular dinner guest, but ended up helping out by delivering tarts or cleaning baking trays during the busy periods leading up to the village fairs, First Holy Communion, Christmas and the Feast of Saint Nicholas.

On Sundays he played the church organ and on weekdays he gave piano lessons to the daughters of families whose money stretched further than the bread, milk and coal bills. When the 'director', as the music teacher was called, was too busy to attend rehearsals, he also filled in as conductor of the brass band.

Sebastian wanted to play music with the sisters as well. Since the house attached to the bakery was too cramped for a piano, he taught Camilla mandolin and Anne violin. He taught the other sisters new songs and new arrangements of songs they had sung before. He played the mouth organ, and together they mounted impromptu concerts in the red-tiled courtyard between the bakery and the house. Young people from the neighbourhood came by to sing along or accompany them on recorders, guitars and accordions. When the courtyard got too crowded, they moved the chairs out onto the street. The neighbours would come out of their houses to listen, sing and clap along. The gloom of everyday reality lifted, and Sebastian filled the air with carefree tunes until the dust was dancing and everyone had forgotten the hard-packed melancholy that was still visible in the gaps between the cobblestones.

In the house of the seven sisters, Sebastian found all the women he had searched for in his life. Together they filled the empty rooms of the house he had inhabited with his grandmother.

He looked up to Martha like the mother he had never known. She represented the security he had longed for as a child. Clara, Camilla and Vincentia were the little sisters who hadn't been there for him to wrestle with. Laughing and swearing under his breath, he chased after them when they ran off with the key to his bike lock. They embarrassed him with remarks about his strictness, things like his habit of combating their habitual disorder by arranging the cutlery neatly to the left and right of the plates. When Sebastian joined them for meals, the knives, forks and spoons were all exactly one quarter of an inch from the edge of the table.

Christina and Anne were the young girls he had never dared to look at. He blushed at the things they said and was too shy to answer. Their presence went straight to his head, and in the dance hall he danced with them wildly until the last echo of the music had left for home.

Marie was like an aunt who asks you a dozen times whether you would like some sugar in your coffee and then forgets to pour it – after which you do it yourself and top up hers while you're at it. Her eccentricities warmed his heart. He cherished the initialled handkerchief she had embroidered for him – he kept it for Sunday best.

While he was visiting them, every woman had her own place and his life was complete, but the moment he was back in his cubbyhole at the presbytery, the women began bickering inside his head. In his thoughts they argued about which kind of love was the most important, and he was unable to decide whether his feelings for the elder sisters were worth more than his attraction to the younger ones. Things might have been simpler if the women had entered his life one after the other, but he had met them all more or less simultaneously and did not know how to react. His body was bombarding him with bewildering messages that made it impossible for him to see the difference between his feelings for an aunt and a sister – and just thinking about the girls on the verge of womanhood was enough to throw his thoughts into complete disarray. He spent long and difficult nights alone in his tiny room.

It was Martha who – totally unexpectedly – put an end to Sebastian's dithering.

Late one Friday afternoon, she came to the small room at the rear of the presbytery with a shirt the ragman had given Sebastian. Although American-made, the shirt had turned yellow with age. It had come with a batch of goods the shopkeeper had bought on the black market, but was not the kind of shirt anyone in the village would buy. It had three small pleats on either side of the buttons and an upright collar with turned-down points. Sebastian loved it and wanted to wear it while conducting the men's choir during a regional competition in the cathedral in the city. He had shown it to Martha and, as he had expected and hoped, she had known how to make it so white that you couldn't look at it without squinting.

For three days she had soaked the shirt in bleach, which she renewed every morning and evening. Martha was elated to see that even the shadows of the brown stripes on the creases had dissolved during the last soaking. Unable to wait to see Sebastian's reaction to his new dress shirt, she decided to take it to him immediately.

She had visited Sebastian at home before and – unfamiliar as she was with the custom of knocking before entering – now walked straight into his room at a time when Sebastian could hardly have been less prepared for a female visitor. He had just had his Friday-afternoon bath in the presbytery and was still glowing hot from the bathwater. He was only wearing underpants.

They were both shocked by this mistimed encounter, and time stood still while they saw things in a way they had never seen them before. Martha stared at the body of a creature she had only known with clothing on. Although aware that men were anatomically different from women, she was still overcome by the virility of the body before her. She stared at the well-built torso for an eternity and felt an immense longing to burst into tears and press herself against that body in an attempt to absorb some of its strength, to become stronger herself and better able to cope with her life. Finally she shook her head and started the clock ticking again by holding out Sebastian's shirt.

'It's completely white,' she said. 'Try it on. If the sleeves are too long, I'll take them up.'

Her words brought Sebastian back to earth, and he tried to concentrate on the shirt that had once seemed so important. Slowly he slipped into the white material and the still-present smell of chlorine. The shirt-tail fell over his woollen underpants, the cuffs hung down over his fingers. Martha tugged at them.

'Yes, a big piece has to come out. I'll take it to the tailor,' she said.

'That's not necessary,' whispered Sebastian. 'I'll wear it with armbands.'

'No, that would be a shame. It needs altering. Take it off again,' she commanded.

Sebastian hesitated. His arms dangled beside the body that had so confused Martha. They were incapable of conveying his hands to the buttons that were waiting to be undone. He stared at the woman, and his eyes pleaded with her to leave him.

Martha refused to accept any such message. One by one, she slid the mother-of-pearl buttons through the buttonholes, starting at the top, until the shirt had fallen open and she was again gazing at his tanned skin.

'You smell so good,' she said softly.

Sebastian breathed in deeply but could only smell the delicate perfume of the talcum powder Martha puffed under her arms and between her legs every morning to stop her skin from chafing. He felt a stirring in his groin and turned his back. He still didn't know whether or not to take off the shirt.

'I'll take it to the tailor myself,' he mumbled. 'I don't have anything else to do today anyway.'

He wanted her to go away, he wanted to be alone to struggle with all his women until he was too tired to think about them any more – but Martha cautiously took the shirt by the collar and peeled it down over his shoulders.

'Men smell different to women,' Martha said, surprised that it had taken her so long to discover such a simple thing.

'Do . . . do they?' he stuttered and began to sweat. The rough tricot of his underpants was taut. He started trembling and inhaled a scent of flowers on the verge of wilting. He turned to face Martha and saw his fingers moving over the buttons of the blouse which was giving off the smell of flowers.

Their breath mingled. Martha felt her breasts jump to attention in her worn brassiere. Without taking her eyes off Sebastian, she lay the shirt to one side.

Sebastian blushed when she touched the hair on his chest. His nipples hardened. The image of his grandmother disappeared, he was no longer able to picture a mother either, and there were no more sisters. Only one woman was left, one total woman.

'How brown you are!' said Martha.

'I go swimming in the river,' he answered, 'and lie in the sun to dry.'

'So down there, you're still white,' mumbled Martha, pointing at the waistband of his underpants.

How many nights had he lain awake thinking of milk-white, almost translucent female bodies and longing to see what they really looked like? He took off her blouse and let it drop to the floor, and the yellowed bra too, and he saw her white breasts with their pink nipples hanging above her white stomach. He laid a hand on the soft flesh of her left breast and felt its warmth flow through his whole body and reach boiling point in his groin.

She unbuttoned her skirt and let it drop.

It was his first time too and afterwards he played the organ better than ever. The entire congregation noticed and people started coming more often – the church was even full for vespers, which delighted the priest because in other parishes church attendance was already falling.

Sebastian's dreams became less tormented. He still loved all seven sisters, possibly even more than before, but now all the women in his thoughts were united in this one woman, and he no longer worried about how to rank them. He now had the peace of mind to concentrate on music and other things of beauty. He became the director of the theatrical society and rehearsed the amateurs until their acting was as convincing as real life. He was appointed permanent conductor of the brass band and moved the village musicians to such heights that the local music association won prize after prize at regional competitions. He was not paid for his efforts, at least not in hard cash, but his achievements were worth far more than any wages the theatrical society or music association could have afforded. He was invited to so many meals that he never needed to cook, and he could spend whole evenings at the café without spending a penny, since he was offered drink after drink and no one ever gave him a chance to buy a round. The brewer's oldest sister gave him an expensive bicycle with drum brakes – she had bought it in the city but was too scared to learn how to ride. Widows gave him their deceased husbands' clothes, and he took them to the tailor's to be altered. Sebastian became increasingly popular with his fellow villagers and wanted for nothing.

Everyone noticed that Martha was smiling more often and had become livelier, but only Christina's perceptive eyes saw the depth of true joy dancing in her sister's laugh. Martha was as disciplined as ever, but less strict with her sisters, who noticed that she was suddenly especially anxious to do the shopping in the village. Much to the amusement of her sisters, she had also developed an acute case of piety and attended church at every opportunity, although she still treated Sebastian exactly as before when-ever he visited the house.

Martha changed physically. She stood straighter, her breasts became fuller and her hips rounder. She went to the city to buy a bra of shining satin and a corset of gleaming damask, with ribs and laces to pull it tight. More and more often she pushed away the unsold tarts the sisters ate them-selves because freezers hadn't been invented and it was a shame to throw them away. Despite her efforts, her belly was soon stretching the material of her pinafore dress. Things no one speaks about have an uncanny way of spreading until their presence covers a village like an invisible cobweb. One day the assistant priest came and spoke to Martha in the living room, the room where years later Sebastian would be laid out in a pair of striped pyjamas. The priest had sent his assistant to talk to Martha because Sebastian's position as organist had become impossible now that everyone knew that he was the father of the child she was expecting.

They married one month after Martha's thirtieth birthday. Sebastian was yet to turn twenty-five. There was no special ceremony. Martha and Sebastian simply went to the sacristy between the seven-thirty Mass and the eight o'clock Mass so that the priest could bless their union. Martha had not bought a new dress for the occasion; she hadn't even bothered to take off her pinafore, but it didn't show because she kept her wide overcoat on the whole time.

From that day, Martha and Sebastian slept together in the double bed that had been discreetly moved into the front room. This room had been the domain of Marie and Anne, but they now moved up to the attic, in turn displacing the journeymen bakers – who were now faced with a choice between finding a boarding house or sharing the attic above the bakery with the mice and the mealworms. Life seemed to settle back into a normal routine, even though everyone knew that nothing could be the same again – something that should never have happened had happened, and the sisters resented the way Sebastian had exchanged his special place in their lives for an everyday chair at the table.

Two weeks after Sebastian moved in, Christina and Vincentia came home with a pink cradle, which they assembled next to Martha's bed. Vincentia left the room without a backward glance while Christina lovingly draped a canopy over the faded angel at the head of the cradle. When Christina showed it to her, Martha nodded and put on a clean pinafore. It was time for her to serve in the shop.

Even before the moment of my birth, I regretted choosing these people for my parents. When my soul was in that region between light and life, looking for a place to develop itself, I had allowed myself to be seduced by Sebastian's magnificent organ playing. I saw his love for things of beauty and was attracted by his passionate acting and inspired direction of the theatrical society, by his talent for breathing life into the most bizarre characters and making them seem as if they really existed. I had not noticed that he lived in a world of dramatic illusion where the responsibility for everything that happened was always fobbed off onto others.

My reasons for choosing Martha were the same as Sebastian's. I felt her strength and her urge to seize life by the horns. But I had not noticed that she was most satisfied when making others happy or that she tended to bear the weight of others' problems. I hadn't seen how tense her shoulders were or realized that she suffered from chronic neck ache.

When Sebastian made cautious attempts to lay his hand on me – there in the hideaway I would be forced to leave in just a few months' time – Martha pushed away his arm. And when he tried to nestle up against us in bed with his strong-smelling body, Martha wriggled away, sometimes even pushing me up against the wooden edge of the bed. I began developing an aversion to life.

Three months after the simple ceremony in the sacristy, I came into the world screaming. When it was time for me to leave my warm home, I fought with Martha for two whole days, but in the end I had no choice but to continue along the path I had chosen. I was forced into the narrow passage, and when I came out it was so cold that I have had to wear flannel vests ever since. For forty days and forty nights I cried. I cried until my tears were exhausted and my battered lungs refused to supply any more air for pointless screaming. Years passed before I cried again. I had poured out almost my entire supply of tears – just to get it over and done with.

From the cradle next to the bed Martha shared with Sebastian, I kept the whole house awake. In the morning everyone grumbled over breakfast with bags under their eyes. Christina wondered whether Martha had enough milk, and Marie suggested that it might even be coming out sour. Anne thought I might have nappy rash – although there were no signs of it – and decided to start rinsing my nappies in a mixture of flour and water. Clara and Vincentia kept their distance, whereas Camilla could spend hours rocking me in her arms as if I were a doll – I was actually a little smaller than her doll and she would often dress me in its clothes. All the attention being paid to the problem she had brought into the house only made Martha nervous.

Whenever Sebastian picked me up to try to stop my screaming, one of the sisters would quickly take me away from him. He never had a chance to grow accustomed to my smell – he was not allowed to feel my skin and he was unable to whisper any words of comfort in my ear. I've spent my whole life trying in vain to remember the things he might have said.

As soon as I was born, Martha resumed her familiar rhythm – up early, opening the shop, loading up the wagon, taking orders, arranging terms with the miller, and discussing overdue bills with her stomach between her knees. I became a new background harmony in the music of the bakery, but my arrival had no effect on the tempo.

When I finally stopped crying, peace returned to the house, but not to Sebastian. His day-to-day presence had tarnished the dreams he had evoked. The sisters began avoiding him.

After just five months, Sebastian could bear it no longer. He left with one change of underwear and his mouth organ. He abandoned everything else, including his stool at the church organ. For the first time in years there was no organ music for High Mass, not even a choir. A week later, everyone was subjected to the wooden thumping of club-footed Johanneke, the youngest daughter of the notary. The magnificent organ suddenly seemed crippled as well – the once so stirring melodies of Bach and Handel emerged hacking and coughing from the pipes. The organ never recovered from the rancour left by Sebastian's departure.

In time everyone forgot why I was even there and went back to the pattern Martha had woven thirteen years earlier when her own father disappeared from one day to the next, leaving her behind to care for six sisters and the small bakery.

Three

The father of the seven sisters was a cheerful fellow, the kind of man who likes to cuddle up to the good things in life whenever troubles threaten to leap upon him like so many fleas. And he had a wife who understood. On Sunday morning she left him lying in the warm hollow of their feather bed and didn't wake him until Mass was about to start. She knew that he wanted to delay his arrival in the church until just before the sermon. She also knew that he would be leaning on the bar of the café opposite the house of God before the priest had given the final blessing. He and his companions would drink to the health of all those who deserved it, and to the salvation of those who were beyond the reach of illness because they had been lying in their graves for so many years that they couldn't even remember what alcohol smelt like. Sometimes, when the village was faced with difficult decisions, they would raise a toast to the brewer – who doubled as a councillor. Once Mass was finished, they would often clink glasses with the priest, who came over to wash down the sour taste of the altar wine. As a token of respect for their spiritual leader, they would drink to the saints in niches, who looked down on the churchgoers with stony devotion. There were even times when they based the rhythm of their drinking on the Litany of the Saints, although often enough by the time they got to Saint Anastasia, the cries of 'I'll drink to that!' were stilled because their tongues were swollen and even their vocal cords had had enough.

Martha's mother knew that alcohol whets the appetite and that her husband would reappear at a predictable hour, leaning against the door jamb or lying on the step about to fall asleep. She left the meat braising so that she could dish it up the moment he came in. There may have been next to no nutritional value left in the beef, but it tasted all the better for it. After his meal, her husband would fall into a deep sleep – that too was predictable – from which he would not awake until the following morning, when it would be time for him to embark on a new week that would inspire him to another errant Sunday.

Husband and wife seldom discussed unavoidable matters such as the payment of electricity, wood and coal bills. He preferred to act as if things like that did not exist, and as long as he provided her with enough money, she had no grounds to remind him otherwise. They understood each other without words.

Martha's parents married when he was twenty-eight and she had just turned nineteen. They were lonely and far from home. This brought them together, but it had nothing to do with love. Three years after their simple wedding, which was not attended by either family since both of them had left home so long before that neither felt obliged to invite anyone, she became pregnant with their first child – just in time to defuse the increasingly bloated gossip about her fertility and his potency. Until then, she had always felt obliged to mumble something about miscarriages (which she had never had) in order to avoid any aspersions on her husband's capacities.

They had their first child baptized Martha Maria and called her Martha for short. Her father was still working in a bakery in the city at that time. Every day he climbed onto his bicycle at four in the morning and didn't come back until late afternoon. A little over a year after Martha, Marie Anne was born. Good Catholic custom dictated that each child be given at least two names, and one night, fuddled with cheap gin, the parents decided to give each following child the second name of the previous child. Marie Anne was called Marie for short. The next child – born three years later – was baptized Anne Christina and called Anne. Christina Vincentia was the fourth child, and was followed by Vincentia Clara. Last to be born were the twins, Clara Camilla and Camilla, who was not given a second name.

Martha, the eldest, did not take after her parents at all. She never learned to dodge unpleasant things the way her father did. But neither did she understand her mother's relaxed approach to life. Martha's parents had talents that they did not pass on in the genes they gave their first-born daughter. Instead, it seems likely that they gave her an inheritance consisting of all the fears they themselves did not want to be burdened with. This would explain why Martha was so much more anxious and timorous than the six sisters who followed her. Her greatest fear was that her sisters might be unhappy, and making sure they weren't became her mission in life.

Marie, the second daughter, was the opposite of her elder sister. She was a fragile-boned child with pale skin and delicate fingers that were suited only to fine embroidery. Unlike Martha, she never worried about the happiness of others.

Anne, the next-born, was shy and silent. She did not start talking until it was time for her to start primary school. She treated words – and feelings – like hard-earned savings.

Christina gathered up all the cheerfulness her sisters had neglected to collect at the entrance to this world. She was lively and full of questions, but always got the answers so mixed up and confused that her own stories, although fun to listen to, were invariably a jumble of contradictions and inconsistencies.

After four daughters, their father's hopes for a son were becoming increasingly desperate. Instead, Vincentia was born, a tomboy who loved the outside air and couldn't stand the heat of the bakery or the tedium of filling tarts.

Clara, the first of the twins, would have made a good boy as well. She was the only one in the family to take after their father. Like him, she avoided problems – but she lacked his fiery temperament. She kept her innermost feelings to herself and had nothing in common with her twin sister, who was lost in the realities of this world.

Camilla was an elfin child, born with hair that was already long enough to take ribbons. She held on tight to the echoes of her mother's cries during the labour and spent every solitary moment listening to the shrieks of women in pain.

*

For years after the arrival of their third child, the girls' mother successfully avoided pregnancy – not that she refused her husband access to her bed: no, she had her own means of contraception and, even though they never discussed it, it was a method her husband did not object to at all. They both knew that his earnings at the bakery in the city were not enough to support a large family, and neither of them wanted any added responsibilities or limitations. They had a good life, and there was no reason for it not to continue in a similar vein for many years to come.

When Anne was six and attending primary school, the village bakery went on sale and her father, who still climbed onto his bike at an ungodly hour every morning to ride to work, remembered a dream he had once shared with his wife. In his dream, they ran a bakery with seven journeyman bakers who kneaded the dough and got the bread out of the oven while they stayed cuddled up together in bed until dawn. With this appealing vision fresh in their minds, they decided to buy the bakery.

As all three of their daughters were already going to school, their mother would have time to fill in for the seven bakers until the business was up and running. But just when it could hardly have been less convenient, a new pregnancy began that was more difficult than any of the previous ones. It seemed unlikely that the baker's wife would be able to help in the new business. Martha was a diligent pupil at the village school, where her marks were so high that she had skipped grades two and four. Only ten years old, she sat among adolescents from the highest grades who giggled about things she didn't understand. She felt shut out. She also knew that once she had finished school she would have to go to work for strangers – maybe even living in – a prospect that crept through her dreams like a wet dog. Sometimes she would go to church to pray to Our Lady of Perpetual Help for a new law that would keep her at school for longer. Such a law *was* in the planning, but it and others like it would come too late for Martha – neither Mary's virginity nor any of Her other qualities were able to hurry it along. The Virgin Mary answered Martha's prayers in Her own way.

One evening Martha's father asked if she would like to help in the bakery after leaving school. Martha said yes straight away, although she could not have guessed what was in store for her. She did not know the meaning of hard work: her mother was an industrious woman who generally had the housework done by the time the girls came home from school. She would give them a glass of lemonade and a slice of gingerbread, then send them off to play among the stacks of timber at the sawmill. Martha was only a child when her father asked her whether she wanted to work in the bakery. As carefree as an infatuated teenager, she committed herself to a life that would have taxed a grown woman.

Martha was still going to school when the family moved into the house next to the bakery. For the first few months, she delivered the bread by bicycle before the school bell rang. At lunchtime, she sold the steaming loaves from the second round of baking in the front room that had been converted into a shop. Sales were minimal at first – their predecessor had neglected his customers – but as soon as Martha was home all day, she began a variety of sales campaigns. She made posters with special offers to stick up in the windows, and once a month she raffled off a tart among the customers who bought two or more loaves of bread a day. She spoke to the customers who bought flour to bake their own bread at home in the wood-burning ranges that people had in their kitchens in those days, and offered them a discount if they brought their dough to the bakery for her father to bake. This proved to be a time-consuming service: the customers began by asking her to deliver the flour, and soon proved unwilling to bring the dough to the bakery either. After closing up shop in the afternoon, Martha had to visit the remote farmhouses and workers' cottages outside the village to deliver the flour, then pick it up again in the mornings in the form of dough, which was sometimes so poorly kneaded that her father had to put it in the mixer before he could bake it. Afterwards she got back on her bike a third time to deliver the bread.

It was not long before Martha developed a thorough dislike for their customers – they always wanted more for less, and she never dared to say no because the bakery needed every customer and her father flew into a rage whenever his grand plans seemed in danger of being derailed. Sometimes the farmers' wives would make her wait while they mixed the dough. She would be overcome by stomach cramps – she knew her father would be standing at the door waiting and counting the extra minutes he would need to keep the oven burning.

Her father was a strict boss and a hard teacher. He taught

her to make the plaited tops for the tarts without wasting a single roll of dough – if she did, he would rap her fingers until her knuckles stung and it was even harder for her to spread the plaits evenly over the fruit. While mixing the bread dough, he would make her recite the quantities of flour, salt and water until she could drone them off in her sleep. He wanted to be sure she would remember if she ever needed to make bread by herself.

On Sunday morning she had time for the bookkeeping. Each week her father would ask her how much was 'on the slate'. If too much was outstanding, he would get nervous and complain that Martha would reduce them to beggary. His solution was to send her out to the worst debtors on Sunday afternoon to try to collect the money, a task she saw as an absolute horror: she knew that, instead of the wives, she would mostly be met by the men, who were much harder. Her father also sent her to the miller in his stead when there was not enough money to pay cash for their flour order, something that happened all too often in the early days. To resolve this problem, Martha bought the grain direct from a farmer and arranged to pay the miller in kind with bread and the seasonal tarts. A council official taught her accounting and how to keep records for tax purposes, something her father refused to have anything to do with – he considered it ridiculous that people he didn't even know could tell him to keep a check on every penny he earned, just so they could demand a share of it later.

Martha was a fast learner, but she had to work at it. She had to steer a course between her father's outbursts of temper and the wishes of 'their holinesses', the bread buyers. Maintaining the peace on either side was no easy task, but when she succeeded she was happy and contented, and free to bury herself in the novels customers gave her. Wandering through stories that were too beautiful to be true, she pushed open the doors to a shop of her own – one that never smelt of bread.

Meanwhile her mother gave birth to a fourth daughter, Christina Vincentia, nursed her, and stayed in the house as much as possible. Although she never played a role in her husband's business, she provided good meals and dry socks, and at night she made a deep hollow in the double bed in the master bedroom so that her husband could roll against her body to cool the passions he had built up during a day in front of the hot oven. And when the first frosts came, she heated stones in the oven, wrapped them in newspaper and slipped them into the girls' beds to keep their feet warm.

As rickety as the structure of their lives at the bakery may have been, there were still warm corners for them to retreat to, and for four years little changed – until a new parish priest appeared on the scene. Less than three weeks after his ordination, he was sitting at the kitchen table asking the mother of four why she had so few children. He accused the thirty-seven-year-old woman of neglecting her Christian duties and promised to pray for the salvation of her soul. Inasmuch as there was any hope left, he added on his way out, and took the precaution of cancelling the tart order that Martha had so carefully negotiated with his pre-decessor. Her father chewed on his moustache until his lip bled, then sent Martha to the presbytery to discuss matters. He and his wife went to confession, and within a year Martha had another little sister, Vincentia Clara. The twins followed soon after.

Martha's mother's health crumbled under the burden of these last two pregnancies. She was almost forty when the twins came, and the labour lasted for two long days. Besides the drunken, chain-smoking midwife, no one was present. Martha, seventeen years old, was baking bread because her father had walked off down the street to escape the screams of his wife, who just couldn't push out that child – no one knew there were two.

The girls' father dragged his wife's screeches down the street behind him and cursed the priest. The warm hollow in their bed had long since split into two shallow indentations – his wife's protest against his kowtowing to the priest in return for an order of tarts.

When Clara and Camilla were two weeks old, their mother died of childbed fever, an affliction from a bygone era. The boozy midwife had ignored the rules of hygiene and had been in too much of a hurry to wait for the afterbirth. It had been left to Martha to assist her mother, and in her ignorance she had not realized that the placenta was tattered and purulent. She thought that they were always like that and simply buried the muck behind the stable where they would later keep the horse.

Martha had too little time for her feverish mother – it was up to her to feed the twins, but the cow's milk gave them colic that made them scream with pain. After her mother died, she didn't go to the funeral with the others either, because she couldn't leave the babies alone. With the twins in her arms, she stood in the shop doorway and watched the horse-drawn hearse taking her mother's coffin to the graveyard on the outskirts of the village. She saw her sisters following their father in their navy-blue dresses with immaculate white collars, and felt a momentary glow of pride at how respectable they looked. But that feeling soon gave way to tears. The salty stains on her cheeks were temporary, but the loneliness that washed over her would last for ever.

After his wife's funeral, the baker could no longer find his way through time. Martha now had to get up to light the oven before feeding Camilla and Clara. A fortnight later, her father stopped coming to the bakery to knead the dough. Martha had to get up in the middle of the night to mix the dough – she could almost do it in her sleep – and let it rise while feeding the babies with goat's milk she had already boiled for half an hour. She then loaded the baking trays and had exactly one hour to doze in the old tub chair she had placed next to the oven.

Four weeks after the funeral, the father of the seven girls did not appear at breakfast. Martha was sympathetic and let him be, but when he didn't come down for lunch either, she sent Christina up to his room. She came back and told them it was empty.

Their father had rowed away on the tears he had been unable to shed – he had been taught that men don't cry.

*

For one month, Martha waited for him to come back. After turning the next page of the calendar, she took the bicycle and rode to the city to ask her father's former employer for advice about what to do with the bakery. Nine weeks after her mother's death, a journeyman baker arrived to feed the oven, bake the bread and clean the trays in return for food and lodging. Marie had left school long before and spent her time embroidering cloths for the table, the sideboard, the dressing table and the chests of drawers in the bedrooms. Martha told her to take charge of the food as well, and she did, but her cooking was so tasteless that no one would eat it.

Anne was still at the domestic science school at the time of their mother's funeral – she had repeated grade four – but Martha told her that it was time for her to stay home and that she needed to learn to ride the bicycle so that she could take over the bread round. Reluctantly, Anne did as she was told and climbed onto the bike every morning, sometimes before sunrise – she had to wrap layers around her heart to keep out the cold.

They abandoned the complicated system of baking dough for the farmers' wives. From now on, they only baked one kind of bread, and at the end of the month Martha visited all the houses to be paid, because few of their customers paid cash. She hardly ever collected enough to pay all their bills and taxes, but it was always just sufficient to save the bakery from bankruptcy.

On Sundays Martha slept in. After her mother's death, she had stopped going to Mass. She did not set foot in a church at all until Clara and Camilla's First Holy Communion – Marie had embroidered two dresses for the occasion. When Martha sat down in front of the statue of Mary, she felt like she was coming home. She realized that a house doesn't change just because it has fallen into the hands of a bad caretaker, and she began attending first Mass every morning. She was just able to fit it in before opening the shop. It gave her the strength she needed to care for herself and her sisters.

Four

The village where Martha was left behind to look after her six sisters lay at the point where the river, which came from Germany, hooked into the Meuse. The narrow stream passed behind the church and divided the community in two. When the wind blew from the south, the rooster on the steeple of the Gothic church looked out over the monotonous modern part of the village, where street after street of identical houses had been built. They all had the same front door with the same slot for letters, an unknown luxury for the inhabitants of the workers' cottages on the other side of the river. It was so unusual for the postman to have something to slide under a door that he habitually knocked when he did – he knew that mail always unsettled the inhabitants, even good news. He was incapable of delivering a postcard without reading it first, and given half a chance he would read it out loud for the recipient. The postman had two knocks: a light, triple tap for a card or a letter from family, and a serious, heavy rap to warn people to prepare themselves when he had just pulled a message from some official body out of his leather bag. Desperately curious, he would stand around talking in an attempt to discover what news had come in the envelope.

*

When the wind blew from the east, the cock on the weather-vane faced the old village. Here, the latest news always began its rounds by being passed along a bar in one of the five cafés on the church square, each of which was frequented by a different caste of dignitaries or workers after the last Sunday Mass. Sunday afternoon was a time to go over the events of the previous week adding the laughter that had been missing the first time round. At the end of the day, the drinkers wobbled home while the fumes of beer and gin spiralled up past the church weathervane and the shutters of the town hall. The shopkeepers and village worthies kept their balance by trailing their fingers along the fronts of the houses that lined the pavements, but the workers and farmers meandered down frayed streets without gutters. On the village outskirts the houses were too far apart to provide a serviceable railing.

The baker's house stood in the middle of the high street with its twin, the greengrocer's, on its left. Once built as a stately home, there was a coach house on the left of the hall and a kitchen and two large rooms on the right. The previous owner had converted the front room into a baker's shop, but customers still had to enter through the hall. This original shop was sparsely furnished with just a few wooden racks and red-painted tin chests that held the warm smell of freshly baked bread. Later, the sisters extended the shop into the hall, and later still, after self-service had come into fashion, they renovated the coach house as well – by which time almost all of the ground floor was given over to the business.

Behind the house was an enclosed courtyard with the blind wall of the greengrocer's on one side and the brick wall of a neighbouring farm on the other. The bakery proper was a separate building, presumably built much later than the house. There was a stable next to the bakery, and between the oven and the stable there was a narrow room with a big tin bathtub. The heat of the oven warmed both room and water. Everyone was allowed a bath once a week according to a rigid timetable, which also gave them the freedom to stay in the bath until their skin was as wrinkled as Oma's.

Left alone to run the bakery and look after her sisters, Martha was forced to hire a baker or find someone who was willing to do the work in exchange for food and lodging. These journeyman bakers seldom stayed longer than a year as that was as long as most men could stand this thoroughly female household. During the war, when the boys and men were taken off to work in German factories, Martha turned to an elderly farmer who was too old to contribute to the occupier's war machine and had nothing to do on his farm because the Germans had requisitioned his stock. Martha thought that she could teach him how to bake bread, but didn't realize that hands that are used to squeezing the udders of a cow might not necessarily be good at kneading dough. After wasting a month in a vain attempt to teach the farmer, she began doing it herself, together with Christina, who had been thrust into adulthood at an age when most children were still getting used to school.

*

No family members ever came to check on the girls. Martha didn't even know where her parents came from. They had never spoken about their families and she did not have any birth certificates – they only found them later when they turned the attic of the bakery upside down during the big renovation, and by that time no one was interested. Even their parents'marriage certificate was missing: it had been in the inside pocket of the suit their father was wearing when he disappeared off the face of the earth. He had worn that same suit – he only had the one – when, cursing and swearing, he had gone to the town hall with the red and white shutters to register the births of his two youngest children.

Sundays at the bakery were never filled with visits by uncles and aunts who came to drink coffee and discuss things that were of absolutely no importance. By way of compensation, Martha cobbled together rituals of her own. Each Saturday she would set a big pan of boiling water on the stove and keep a hunk of meat simmering until the next day, by which time all the taste and goodness had passed into the water. She would add a packet of vermicelli and let it soak in this hearty stock, and when the mood took her, she would also throw in handfuls of cauliflower florets.

The sisters' Sunday was not complete without this soup. Around four o'clock, they would follow it with a cup of coffee and a slice of tart and would then, weather allowing, go out for a walk. During these strolls, they held hands tightly, as if they were scared that someone might come between them. Martha held the twins' hands, and Christina walked between Anne and little Vincentia, who in turn would take the hand of one of the twins. Marie always followed ten steps behind. The other villagers would see them like this in the Count's woods or in the new suburbs – they were always checking whether any potential customers had moved in – and cyclists would ring their bells frantically until they let go of each other's hands to let them pass. In winter, they crowded around the kitchen stove like kittens and drank hot cocoa into which they dunked gingerbread biscuits. Later, when I started to ask questions about this period, these were the only things they remembered – they knew that troubles build up if you hold onto them for too long and preferred to erase bad things from their memories the moment they happened.

The years before Sebastian's arrival passed slowly but without any great drama. Even the war left them unscathed. As a baby and toddler, Camilla had been afflicted with so many childhood diseases that even their GP had to look some of them up in his textbooks, but during the occupation she turned out to be stronger than most other children. In these difficult years, the sisters did not suffer greatly.

Despite having proved useless in the bakery, the old farmer still dropped by almost every day. At first he would always have some excuse – he'd found a side of bacon, for example, and had fried it up to make thick sandwiches for them – but soon his visits became such a habit that his arrival was eagerly awaited. The old man had the time of his life during the war. His farm was so dull and so far outside the village that even loneliness made a wide detour around it. He was a bachelor and had always lived with his sister, but she had died the year before the German invasion, leaving him alone.

In the last years of the occupation, this changed because his barns and haylofts were full of people in hiding. At night they would sneak into the warm kitchen to eat the bread Martha had given him and the dripping he had scraped out of the pan at the bakery. After the farmer had told them the news from the village and they had eaten all the bread, a thumb-marked pack of cards would appear on the table and they would bluff and cheat and laugh and laugh until morning, when they all disappeared again behind panels and bales of hay.

The farmer – like all farmers – was so stingy that he scraped his bum clean with a piece of wood to avoid wasting a square of newspaper. He wore a tattered shirt, and trousers he had mended himself with gunny patches. He didn't wear underpants. It made no difference that he had three suits hanging in his wardrobe and at least six woollen vests and pairs of long johns he had never worn at all. His cellars were full to bursting with food as his sister had always preserved anything they couldn't eat fresh. He now reluctantly brought these jars and pots to the bakery, where they gave him the right to relax in Grandpa's chair and warm himself on the presence of a borrowed family.

He was killed before changing circumstances would have forced him to give up his newly acquired relatives. On the eve of the evacuation, he was hit by a stray shell. He died immediately. When Martha went to the cellars looking for food to take with them for the evacuation, she found them empty, plundered by the people he had hidden on his land.

Oma was all the family we had. I was less than six months old when she came to live with us. She had appeared at the shop counter one day with a small cardboard case, and the sisters simply assumed that she was Grandpa's mother. Later this turned out to be impossible. We called her Oma because her youthful glory had faded completely and hung in drab locks over her temples. She might have been Grandpa's older sister or aunt, or maybe just the family housekeeper. Perhaps she had nothing to do with the family at all.

Oma moved into the kitchen and looked after me, patiently feeding me the porridge I loathed and giving me salami sandwiches when I was far too young, causing digestive complaints no doctor has ever been able to heal. After lunch, she pushed two armchairs up against each other to make a cot, then sang me to sleep while knitting me woolly hats and prickly woollen underpants. Those pants of hers explain the difficulties the sisters had in toilet-training me; I was in no hurry to move on from my soft, much-washed nappies.

Oma spoke a hotchpotch of dialects in a confused accent. It was possible that she had lived for a time in eastern Belgium in the Voer valley, close to the German border. We never found out. Whenever I asked her where she came from, she gave an evasive answer. Occasionally she did talk about her childhood, but those stories always seemed like something she had read somewhere, although it was far from certain that she could read at all. Sometimes she would announce in a grave voice that she was going to read the paper and then, after leafing through it for several minutes, lay it aside again while pronouncing that newspapers were a waste of good money and newspaper people were full of hot air.

It was nothing short of miraculous that I avoided copying her confused way of talking. Perhaps my aunts made sure to correct me in time.

At five months I was already sitting up. At eight months I was pulling myself up on the spindles of the armchairs, and a month later I was walking through the kitchen. Once a month Christina or Anne would take me to the child health centre, where they would undress me in one of the playpens. Whereas the other babies born in the same month were still blowing spit bubbles and lying flat on their backs on the blankets, I had already scrambled upright and was sticking my head over the top of my enclosure to stare at my peers and chat away in baby talk, telling them stories they had never heard before.

I wasn't a pretty baby. I was bald and I had no eyebrows and my greyish-blue eyes were hidden away in deep folds. I wasn't heart-warming. That didn't change later either; I didn't become an attractive child.

But I was different. And that wasn't temporary either.

I started reading long before other children my age. I suspect that this was due to my aunts' passion for books. When I was still very young, they started giving me books and magazines they kept in the attic.

The sisters were so mad about reading that they became nervous when there was no book or magazine within arm's reach. Any kind of story would do. There were always books lying face down on the box seat of the bread wagon, and the sisters would quickly read on during the short distances between customers, even if one of the other sisters had read the preceding pages. The sisters formed a collective – finishing the book was more important than following the story. Anne even read while knitting and Vincentia would often read while drying the dishes.

Only Marie had no time for letters. She was so addicted to her cross stitches that she became completely word-blind and couldn't even spell her own name.

No one thought of buying picture books for me. Instead I was given back copies of *The Guardian Angel*, a school magazine for young girls; cloying photo novels with the story in balloons; and the *Libelle* - once everyone else had read it. I carefully tore out the pages and screwed them up, then spent hours playing with the balls of paper. Until the day I smoothed out one of my balls and saw a crazed picture of an elf that winked at me when I tugged at the piece of paper. I began conversations with the pictures, and every time they told me a story it was slightly different than the time before, because there were things they had forgotten to mention or because they had got something wrong. This was how I learned to read, and it was a method school-teachers were never able to reward with high marks. They wanted me to read the school books word for word – exactly as they were written. And that was the one thing I never learned to do.

Five

Marie had been going steady for twelve years before I was even born, but marriage was a subject she carefully avoided. Although she met her fiancé when she was just seventeen, she didn't get married until she was in her thirties. The day after war broke out, the couple made their engagement official, as if doing so would somehow thwart Hitler's soldiers, who weren't the least bit interested. Their marriage at the register office exactly two days after the introduction of rationing made even less of an impression on the German troops. As a legally married woman, Marie now had a right to extra rations, even though she continued to live at home with her sisters – the Church would not allow her to share a bed with her husband until she had repeated her marriage vows before God and this was something she refused to do in an occupied country, regardless of the occupying forces' continuing indifference to her marital state. She saved up the coupons for the extra rations so she could sell them later, when everything was in short supply, and use the money to buy sheeting and embroidery silk on the black market in the Belgian border towns. While war raged around her, she embroidered away at her trousseau – even when the air-raid alarm sounded and they had to take shelter in the cellar, she took her sheets with her and passed her needles through the fabric by the flickering light of a candle. After the supply of black-market embroidery silk had dried up, she unravelled old tablecloths to complete her designs. The scenes were invariably religious. She based them on holy cards, but added elements from her own fantasies – and these were drenched with blood.

On one of the sheets, she embroidered the trial of Abraham. She depicted him with a waist-length beard and a raised knife, and every cross-stitch trembled with despair. Although the Bible clearly states that an angel stopped the knife before it touched the throat of Abraham's son Isaac, the border of the sheet was still awash with red cross-stitches.

Marie had embroidered the crucifixion on countless pillowcases, and one day the priest happened to come into the bakery when she was on her way out with her latest piece in her hands. Deeply impressed, he kept on praising her work until she offered to embroider the parish vestments. Marie saw it as a commission from God and began embroidering chasubles and albs with detailed scenes from the four Gospels. She threw herself into her new task with such a passion that it was soon too much for her alone. When Sister Redemptora started up the domestic science school again after the war, the pupils were enlisted to help during craft lessons. The girls began grudgingly and some of them even refused, but all signs of resistance melted away when the bishop arrived with a photographer to check on the progress of the churchly vestments. There is hardly a village photo album of that vintage that doesn't include newspaper photographs of girls holding up their most beautiful pieces of embroidery. Seldom, if ever before, had such impressive vestments been worn in such a small parish.

Everyone wondered why Marie didn't get married, but whenever anyone questioned her about it, she acted as if she hadn't even heard.

Martha put her foot down one evening when the sisters were all at home because none of them had a date with an admirer and there were no rehearsals for the girls' choir. She waited until I was in bed under my US War Relief quilt with a full stomach and smelling of soap, then announced that it was time Marie consecrated her marriage: if she put it off any longer they would soon be celebrating her crystal engagement anniversary. Either way, they could do with a party, she laughed, but added seriously that it was high time for her to get married because otherwise she would be too old to have children. Martha suggested a date just after the autumn fair; it was always quiet in the bakery around then and they would have plenty of time to bake tarts and cakes for the reception. They had to make sure it was a beautiful wedding; after all, she would be the first of the bakery girls to get married (her own wedding having temporarily slipped her mind).

She even had a wedding dress for her sister, a second-hand gown she had accepted in lieu of payment from a pot and pan manufacturer. The man loved money so much that he resented spending it on daily necessities and put off paying his bills so long that the baker, the butcher, the tailor and the shoemaker all began muttering that they would have to stop supplying him. Since he was always careful to choose storekeepers who would be afraid to speak up for fear of losing his custom, things always got way out of hand. Marie had been going on about his eldest daughter's bridal gown for days, so Martha offered to cancel all his debts and throw in the tarts for the fair in exchange for the dress.

But Marie didn't want a second-hand bridal gown. She bought a simple wedding dress and set about embroidering it from neck to hem, which meant postponing the wedding for six months, and another three months after that for the dresses for Clara and Camilla, her bridesmaids. When she had finished those, she started on a white pinafore with flounced shoulders for me, so that I could walk before her as flower girl. She would have liked to have a pageboy as well, dressed up in a black waistcoat embroidered with white flowers, but Martha had had enough and set a date. She sent Marie and her fiancé to the priest to arrange the Mass and invited Marie's parents-in-law-to-be over to meet the family, something that still hadn't happened.

The wedding was just before the summer fair. Marie made an adorable bride, and there wasn't a bachelor there who didn't regret not having courted her more persistently. She wore a white dress that trailed along the ground behind her. The bodice, beneath which Marie wore a padded bra to make up for her flat chest, was embroidered with arum lilies in gleaming white and beige silk; the skirt was covered with petals. Her groom was a prince in a white suit and black dress shoes.

Martha had spent days arguing with Marie about that

white suit: a white wedding wasn't meant to include the bridegroom. Marie had a thousand and one reasons for not marrying a man in black. If black was the colour of the end, she yelled furiously, and of death and mourning, then it couldn't possibly be the colour for starting a new life! She strengthened her case by citing religions all over the globe whose men married in white or red, and even brought up Prince Hendrik's white funeral, until finally Martha's head was spinning and she sulkily told the tailor to start work on a cream suit.

The church was only a few hundred yards from the bakery. The bridal couple could easily have walked, but at nine o'clock that morning a coach and six horses pulled up in front of the house for Aunt Marie, her fiancé, the bridesmaids – Clara and Camilla – and me.

It came as a complete surprise to Martha. She never found out who paid for the coach either. It couldn't have been the groom's family, they had clearly stated that the wedding was the responsibility of the bride's family. They refused to contribute a penny, despite the fact that Marie had lost both her parents.

Behind closed doors and in public places people whispered for years about the white coach with the undertaker at the reins. Rumour had it that he was Marie's real father, that she wasn't the baker's daughter at all; that would have explained why she was so different from the rest of the family. It was true that Marie and the undertaker were strangely intimate, but if they were related in any way they managed to keep it so secret that even the people he buried came no closer to finding out the truth.

The undertaker had painted the coach he usually used for transporting coffins and had rigged up temporary benches in the back for the bridal pair and the bridesmaids. Someone whispered that it was bad luck to ride to your wedding in a hearse, but Marie wasn't listening.

A week later the coach was pitch-black again and carrying the town clerk to his final resting place.

Martha and the other sisters had to walk along behind the coach with the bridegroom's cousins, aunts, uncles and great-uncles, all of whom were complete strangers to us. The girls from the domestic science school lined up on either side of the church door to wave embroidered flowers and sing a song that had been written especially for Aunt Marie. I was so excited I wet myself. My new, store-bought, non-prickly cotton underpants were drenched, and I let the pee run down my leg into my black patent leather shoes. My socks were sopping and squelched when I walked. No one else noticed, and I seemed to be the only one bothered by the smell of urine.

Aunt Marie followed me into the church with her prince and bridesmaids, but my nerves were too fast for them and I got to the priest long before they did. When he stopped me and turned me around, my bladder almost let loose again at the sight of all those beautiful women in embroidered gowns.

A fourth woman wearing a blood-red veil came in behind them. She followed them up to the front and sat down right next to the bride without anyone paying any particular attention to her. As far as I could tell she joined in with all the prayers, but the priest didn't give her communion. After Mass was over, she followed the newly-weds to the Lady chapel where my aunt lit a candle to Our Mother of Perpetual Help. That was the last I saw of the stranger, and amid all the hustle and bustle of the wedding, I forgot to ask what she was doing there in the church.

In village legend, this wedding took on a life of its own. The celebrations lasted two days. With Martha's help, the new journeyman baker had made a wedding cake so big and so sweet that it left everyone licking their lips for weeks. Martha had high hopes that it would become the bakery's new speciality, but no one else ever ordered it.

It was such beautiful weather that everyone could sit outside. The celebrations began in the small courtyard between the house and the bakery, but the guests kept on coming and the courtyard soon became so crowded that everything had to be moved out to the front of the house. When we ran out of tables and chairs, the neighbours went home for more, but with all the cars driving through the village it was no longer possible to sit in the middle of the road like in the old days. The guests sat on the pavement on either side of the street, eating cake and tarts and singing along with the band. People danced until dawn, then went off to work in the factories or to open their own stores. For the first time in its existence, the bakery stayed shut on a weekday, and towards the end of the afternoon everyone dropped by again to talk and savour the cheerfulness one last time. There was still plenty of tarts and salads and braised beef, so the tables were dragged back out. After all the leftovers had been used up, the neighbours brought out smoked sausages and chops and cigars, and the scent of the wedding began spiralling up past the church steeple all over again. The next-door neighbour sang his sad ballads, and everyone sang the refrain with tears in their eyes. And the farmer from the bottom of the valley launched into the song he always sang about a girl who lured her admirer to her bedroom window but neglected to tell him that the guard dog was off the chain. Everyone split their sides laughing at the last verse, when the farmer sang that he'd never be fooled again. Some people had heard the song at least a hundred times, but they still joined in for a rousing conclusion.

> Rosie, Rosie, horrible lass,
> That wasn't very sporting,
> You made me look a terrible ass,
> I'll come no more a-courting.
> I won't come knocking at your door,
> You won't make me one of your fools,
> I learned my lesson and what's more,
> You're not worth the family jewels.

For the second night in a row, they did the conga out in the street, down to the church and back. When the sun rose on the festivities for the second time, everyone went to bed, exhausted from partying. Some people didn't make it all the way to their own beds and crept into other people's or fell asleep in their bedroom doorways or on the bare pavement in front of their houses.

A terrible silence descended over the village. The stores didn't open that day and the machines in the factories were quiet because not enough workers had shown up to run them. A carefree feeling that would be tangible for months was abroad in the village.

The crêpe-paper garlands were left hanging until they went mossy with the autumn dew and started stinking like real flowers that should have been thrown out ages ago.

Six

At first Marie came back home to drink tea with her sisters every Saturday evening around seven, after they had closed the shop. Her husband accompanied her the first few times but it was a twelve-mile round trip and he soon gave up and left her to make the trip alone on her sturdy lady's bike. After three months, she too stopped coming.

Marie's departure left a hole in our lives, but she didn't give it time to heal. Before six months had passed, she was back at her old place at the table. We never again set eyes on the man who had married in white.

Around the time of Marie's wedding the stars were clotted together in a conjunction that upset the entire fabric of life in the sisters' house. So many things happened at once that it took years for Martha to restore order in her household.

The twins finished school just when Marie left home and, since Marie had never made much of a contribution to the housework, there were suddenly too many people for the work that needed to be done.

Martha called a family meeting and announced that Anne should go into domestic service.

*

Anne had never put any love into the fulfilment of her tasks in the shop and on the delivery wagon. She had been born with such a cold heart that only the warmth of people who loved her could keep the blood from freezing in her veins. Her uncomplaining submission to the rituals of the bakery had kept her alive. Outsiders saw her unfailing conformism and took her for a satisfied woman, but that was mere façade. Anne desperately needed a companion.

Martha and Christina were soulmates and shared their joys and sorrows wordlessly. They were so attuned to each other that their thoughts became entangled, and at times neither of them could be sure that the ideas passing through her mind were her own and not the other's. Marie was her own companion and if she fell short of expectations, there was always confession. Vincentia divided her affections between Christina, with whom she discussed adult matters, and the twins, who brought out her childish side. Clara and Camilla had each other. But Anne had no one to bare her soul to or talk with about men, a subject that often occupied her thoughts, for the simple reason that she knew so little about it.

Martha was aware of Anne's horror of contact with the customers and now suggested that she go to work for the mayor instead. The head of the council had told Martha that he was worried about his wife's health and had decided to take a housekeeper. He already had a charwoman to take care of the heavy work in the mayoral residence, and twice a week the washing and ironing was done by a slightly retarded woman who lived with an English pilot who had never returned to his fatherland after the war because he had forgotten his parents' address. The miller's three strapping daughters did the spring cleaning. But there was no one to look after the children, and they needed someone to prepare and serve afternoon tea when visitors came. The mayoress was becoming increasingly forgetful and had begun acting strangely. She let the children sleep in past noon on schooldays and gave them cake with whipped cream for breakfast, while dishing up cheese and treacle sandwiches for her husband's visitors. It was all too embarrassing for the mayor, and he was looking for someone to relieve his wife of these tasks.

The mayor's house was an outbuilding of a German count's chateau. It had originally been built for the game warden, but times had changed and the new gamekeeper found it too large and too grand. A man of simple tastes, he had felt uncomfortable in the stately Graeterhof and had preferred moving to a modest home on the edge of the count's woods with his wife and three sons. Graeterhof stood empty for years – until the new mayor, who made no bones about his admiration for the nobility, requested it as his official residence at the time of his appointment. The elderly count granted his request and did not even ask for rent. Years later, control over the estate passed to the count's granddaughter, who immediately drew up a contract in which she demanded such a ridiculously high rent that the by-this-time ex-mayor packed his bags in a sulk and moved straight into an old people's home in the city. Despite having lost his post to a younger man, he had still hoped to live out his days in Graeterhof.

*

Anne was probably the most beautiful and elegant of the seven sisters. Her wavy, shoulder-length hair was thick and dark, and she almost always wore it down. Her eyes were lighter than her sisters', and at times they looked as if they were made of pure jade. Her nose was beautifully sculpted and she had a striking, symmetrical mouth. Her breasts were so full and so firm that she had no need of a bra, not even in the period when she became addicted to expensive lingerie. Her tummy was slightly rounded, and when she was young that was the height of fashion. Alone among the sisters, she had inherited her mother's slim shapely legs and slender ankles that never swelled up with fluid, a complaint that beset most of the women in the village, sometimes from their early twenties.

With her loneliness pulled tight around her shoulders, Anne left for the mayoral residence. She was given a bedroom to herself, something she found very hard to adjust to – the sisters still slept two to a bed, sometimes even three to a bed. Anne, who had always felt most secure snuggled up against the backside of one of her sisters, suddenly had to sleep alone, between sheets that were washed so often they never had a chance to take on the scent of her body. If she wanted to see her sisters she had to go by bicycle – the mayor's house was outside the village.

But her new life was warmer than her sisters' bums. It even began to seem as if the long bike ride and the unfamiliar smell in the folds of the sheets were helping her to feel at home at the mayor's. She learned how to get along with children, something that came naturally to her. The mayor's children were sweet-natured, if somewhat lacking in character, a tendency that probably came from their mother's side. The eldest child had a piano lesson at home once a week, and Anne would accompany him on the violin during practice. She learned about gardening from the gardener, who began by being reticent about telling her too much about the growth and blossoming of herbs and plants, anxious not to endanger his own position. However, he soon realized that the garden was much too big for a woman who had never dug the earth.

New values entered Anne's life. And something unforeseeable happened: she fell in love with the mayor.

Christina too began to see life in a new light. While her sister was losing her heart to the mayor, she was falling in love with the owner of a garage on the highway.

Like the river, the highway cut through the community, connecting the village to the city in the south and a series of smaller villages in the north. The garage owner with whom Christina was to share such beautiful feelings was twenty years her senior and had never been married. He had a contract with a local bus company and employed two mechanics to repair their buses. Since these vehicles were complete wrecks, the mechanics were often sent out to fix them wherever they had broken down. At first this was only along the route of the bus service, but later the company branched out into excursions to the Belgian Ardennes and the Ruhr in Germany, and the mechanics were obliged to travel further and further to repair the coaches. They sometimes took me along for the ride and taught me to eat bratwurst in Germany and chips with mustard pickle in Belgium.

The garage owner was a kind man with a long horsy face and pale blue eyes. He had an apologetic laugh and always smelt of motor oil, even when he had just had a bath and was wearing his Sunday best.

Christina and the horse-faced garage owner fell for each other one day when she delivered a birthday cake. The garage owner had ordered the cake for his mother's sixtieth birthday, and Martha had cycled all the way into town to buy marzipan roses and a decoration saying 'Congratulations Mother'. Christina, who was doing the bread round alone that day and in a hurry, tripped on an extension lead on her way into the garage and dropped the cake onto the oily cement floor. Cream splashed up onto the walls and marzipan roses flew through the air and ended up stuck on car windscreens, the workbench and the filthy windows.

One rose stuck to the garage owner's overalls. He stared down at it with astonishment until it came loose and fell to the floor. The man with the friendly, horsy face bent forward to look at the wilted marzipan and began to cry. Silently at first – tears ran down his cheeks and left white furrows in the dirt on his face – then more and more disconsolately. He sobbed that it was the first time in his life that he had ordered a cake, that on this special birthday he had wanted to make a gesture to thank his mother for all the years she had cared for him, and similar sentimental nonsense. He didn't know where to turn to hide the tears that had come out of nowhere.

Christina had never seen a man cry before. She looked

on in shock, and had to suppress an urge to dry his tears with the corner of her apron. She felt that it was a delicate moment for this man, who might not have cried since he was a boy. She hesitated. No one had ever taught her how to cope with the sorrow of men. Finally she could only think of one thing to do: she wiped the tears away with her fingertips, smearing strange shapes in the black lines on his cheeks.

The tears stopped out of sheer amazement, and the grease monkey gave her an embarrassed smile. He said that he would live after all, and Christina stammered that she would be back with a new cake.

Early the next morning she arrived with a cake that she and Martha had baked that night – this time without roses – and stayed on to drink coffee with the family and neighbours until the cake was almost finished. In the weeks that followed, she kept on dropping in. She manufactured all kinds of excuses to stop to talk to the garage owner for more than a few minutes, and the garage owner ordered more bread and tarts than he needed. Even if his mother had made enormous cut lunches for the mechanics to take on their trips to the broken-down coaches, they would still have had too much bread. Christina never dared to ask what they did with it all.

The horse became so used to resting at the garage that it even stopped when Christina was planning on hurrying along to the next customer and dropping in on her way home at the end of the day. It would look back at her questioningly, and Christina would need to crack the whip to get the indignant animal moving again.

*

The garage owner fished around for excuses to keep Christina in his vicinity as well. He decided that tour companies could order fruit buns and rock cakes from the sisters to give or sell to their customers. They spent days discussing this plan. They always found something to talk about, even if some of the subjects were so ridiculous that the garage owner began to chuckle with embarrassment and Christina's hearty laugh pealed through the garage, imbuing such a sense of glee that for hours afterwards the garage owner was unable to wipe the smile off his face.

They talked until they were thoroughly used to each other. Everyone took their engagement for granted and no rings were needed.

After leaving school, the twins were put to work in the bakery. Martha had come up with a plan to keep the work from becoming too monotonous. The girls were to spend alternate weeks helping in the bakery and on the wagon. Generally, two of the sisters went out on the bread wagon to do the deliveries – each doing one side of the street. The twin that had done the deliveries for a week would spend the next week in the shop or helping the bakers.

The household chores were allocated randomly as an extension of the other jobs. The bakers generally cleaned the baking trays and the mixer, and one of the girls would scrub the red tiles of the bakery. Oma looked after the kitchen, and whoever was serving in the shop mopped the floor. But anywhere that didn't need to be swept and mopped daily could be neglected for weeks at a time. Since none of the sisters liked cleaning, they would sometimes all join in together to do it of a Sunday afternoon. It was only when they suddenly noticed sticky grey strands in their dark hair or when the sunshine revealed a foggy layer stuck to the windows, that they would realize it was time to brush away the cobwebs, fill the buckets and take up the sponges and chamois. They would be overcome by an attack of cleanliness so intense it resembled a ritual purification.

They began by first drawing the curtains to prevent the neighbours from observing their transgressions against the Church's day of rest, something that would definitely have been reported to the priest, who would no doubt have come up with appropriate measures to punish them. In the twilight of the seventh day, they scrubbed the glaze from the tiles and polished a layer of glass off the window panes; they cleaned the linoleum in the bedrooms by sanding it back with Vim. At the end of the afternoon, when all their muscles were aching, they brought out a bottle of gin. Everyone fourteen and over was allowed a shot of gin, and on cleaning days they invariably kept pouring until the bottle was empty.

Seven

When Marie came back home, she wasted no time on explanations but simply lugged her chests of embroidered linen up to the attic and resumed her old place at the table. She pushed me out of Christina's bed, where I had been allowed to sleep since her departure, and went back to embroidering. Her needle pierced the fabric with even greater enthusiasm. She received more and more commissions from people seeking wedding gifts for daughters or nieces. Although cleansed of blood, the scenes were as detailed as ever.

Marie almost never went out on the baker's wagon, but one day she offered to help Christina with the bread round because her bicycle had a flat tyre and she needed to deliver a set of bed linen to a farmer. Marie's help amounted to watching a horse that never wandered and letting Christina take care of the deliveries. These could take a very long time as some customers, especially the ones who lived far outside the village, insisted on hearing the latest gossip before giving their order. Sometimes they wanted to know what had been happening in the city as well because they were too stingy to buy a newspaper. They gave the sisters mugs of scalding cocoa or coffee so that they would have plenty of time to tell them stories while they were waiting for it to cool off, and in cold weather the young women were only too happy to give in to temptation. What was more, the customers had stories of their own to get off their chests. Stories about family feuds, annoying neighbours, home remedies and the diseases they cured, and stories about men and women who went to bed with each other despite being married to someone else. It was only much later that I realized why some children were treated so strangely. Everything might have happened in the dark, but that didn't stop the word from spreading all over the village, and bastards just happened to have a different status to legitimate children. No one explained things like that and I never understood why I wasn't allowed to talk to Jacques, the boy who lived next to the practice hall. It was only when Jacques himself was a hazy memory that I heard he was the son of the new baker, whereas his mother lived to celebrate her silver wedding anniversary with the tobacconist.

The sin that had preceded my own birth was long forgotten. Each sister had taken part of it upon herself until finally no one knew whose child I actually was.

It was bitterly cold the day that Marie went out on the wagon. The mist crept past the wheels and under the blankets she had laid over her legs. She shivered and was tormented by visions of steaming cocoa. Just when she was about to jump down to go and see what was keeping her sister, the horse took a step forward to reach some chestnut leaves. The wagon jolted, and Marie stumbled and caught her foot in the reins. She hit her head on the tree as she fell, and when Christina came out minutes later, she found her lying unconscious on the ground.

I no longer remember if I loved Aunt Marie when I was little. I was only four when she had the accident and the resulting concussion led to unbearable headaches that afflicted her for the rest of her life. She had been back home for almost two years when it happened. I was often sent upstairs to keep her company when she was confined to bed with yet another splitting headache, and at such times we both suffered. Her tight-lipped expression sealed my own lips and I couldn't think of anything to say to distract her. I couldn't even remember the stories from my balls of paper. I felt that her suffering went beyond a pounding in her skull; pain seemed to wrack her whole body, even if Vincentia said that she was just a malingerer: her headaches were always worst in the lead-up to holidays . . .

Aunt Marie and I did not understand each other. Mostly I talked with Christina, and when she had time, she read me stories no one had ever written. Later, when I could read myself and went looking for those dragons and witches in her books, I discovered that they no longer lived there. Christina was also the only one I could talk to about boys. With Clara and Camilla that was impossible. It would have made more sense, but with a twelve-year difference in our ages, we were too far apart to be friends and too close to have an aunt–niece relationship.

Anne often took me with her when she went to the city to buy lace bras and panties. She would ask me what I thought, and since I knew that she wanted to hear that

I thought she looked beautiful, that was what I told her. Sometimes she'd give me a ride on the back of her bike to the mayor's house, where she tried to get me to play with his children. This was never a success – I had never learned how to play with other children. They only started to like me later, when I was able to learn poems off by heart and recite them.

Vincentia took me with her whenever she had to pick up something with the wagon after the bread round. Sometimes she made the horse gallop so that the wagon would rock dangerously and I would be frightened and hold on tight to the box. I remember her eyes gleaming while she cracked the whip and told me that Indians were chasing us. She told me that she had learned how to talk to horses. I believed her: the horses weren't the same when she was around. I tried to talk to them myself but none of the horses I knew could understand me. I never learned to love horses. The truth was that I never stopped being afraid of them – they were so big.

When the horse needed shoeing, Vincentia would perch me on its massive back and lead it to the smith on a loose rein. My crotch would hurt because my short legs were spread too far and I was always glad when we made it to the smithy by the railway tracks.

Early on Sunday mornings, before the bells rang for the first Mass, Vincentia went riding on Wood Hill. She used the saddle Sebastian had left behind. The brewer had had the saddle made especially for him in England, but had given it to Sebastian after realizing that he was less keen on riding than he had thought. My father had taught Vincentia to ride the bakery horse. Whenever they had a chance, they would borrow the brewer's horse and gallop together for hours over the heath, returning with froth-covered mounts. Martha had thrown out everything else that reminded her of Sebastian, but she had allowed Vincentia to continue using his saddle.

Eight

I started infant school the autumn after Aunt Marie's accident. On the first day the twins took me to the playground and handed me over to Miss van der Beek, who sat me down in a classroom and left me to tensely await developments. For weeks the thought of starting school had been weighing me down like a stomach full of wet sand. I hadn't been able to eat properly, and my diarrhoea had been even worse than usual.

The school building was next to the convent and the yard was closed off by a green-painted iron fence with a big gate in the middle. Behind that fence, the mystery of writing would be revealed to me. My crumpled balls of paper would be transformed into magical volumes. Inside that building, I would gain access to a new science that would allow me to transcend myself. Such a thing could only be possible through the mediation of a nun, because in my eyes nuns were extraterrestrials. Here my world would be expanded, here I would meet children my own age . . .

After Miss van der Beek had placed a child behind each desk – boys by the windows, girls by the wall – she pulled the door shut. She told us that she was our teacher and that she was going to teach us nice things. I was astonished to see a normal woman standing there instead of one of those enigmatic beings whose black-and-white clothes hid everything except a face and two pale hands. I had gone to school expecting to be taught by one of those mysterious creatures, not by a pointy-breasted woman in a tight pullover and a straight, pleated skirt. But the school had two infant classes and the nun had led off other children.

The woman standing at the front of the classroom where I was now expected to spend a large part of my day opened a cupboard, took down a plank with big blocks of grey clay and told us all to come up and fetch one. I took one of the sticky lumps, deposited it on my desk and watched with horror as the boys began squeezing the filthy mass in front of them through their avid fingers. I almost vomited. The woman picked up a lump of clay herself, broke some off and rolled it between her palms until it was a round ball. She showed it to us, then made a larger ball, stuck the little one on top, and drew a face on it with a piece of wood. 'You can make a man like this,' she said, 'and if you like, you can give him arms and legs and a hat. Try it.'

My hands lay paralysed in my lap. They refused to touch the clay a second time. Miss van der Beek walked between the desks. When she saw that I hadn't done anything with my wet grey lump, she squatted beside me, broke off a piece of clay and tried to lay it in the palm of my right hand. I hurled it across the room. The teacher did not understand me. I couldn't explain it to her. She spoke another language and used words I had never learned. All I could do was whisper 'dirty'. Most of the children had stopped what they were doing and were looking at us. I heard their giggles and wanted to cry, but I didn't have any tears and all that came out was a painful, dry hiccup from deep in my chest.

'There's nothing to look at,' said the teacher, 'go back to work.'

She left me sitting there, walked past the other desks, helped children to make other shapes, and finally told us to knead the clay back into one big lump, make it into a block and then press a hole into it with our thumbs. Once everyone had brought their lump back to the plank, she used a watering can to pour a little water into each thumb-hole. She looked at me and saw that I was still sitting motionless behind my lump of clay. She waited for a moment before asking the girl in front of me to return my clay. Afterwards we had to go to the toilets to wash our hands. When we came back, she wrote something on a piece of paper and brought it over to me. 'Give this to your mother,' she said. I gave the note to Oma, who stuffed it into her apron pocket and promptly forgot about it, so that it eventually dissolved in the wash.

The rest of the morning we drew with coloured pencils. That was more fun and I almost forgot my disappointment about having a teacher who was like my aunts. But after the lunch break I didn't want to go back.

I hadn't counted on Oma, who ignored my stamping and shouting, took me by one arm and dragged me back to school, where she plonked me down in my desk and forbade me with a steely gaze from budging until the bell rang.

*

The second day was a repeat of the first, ex
clay was replaced with white glue in a jam jar.
Beek told us to cut strips of coloured paper an
how to turn them into rings by dipping a l
glue, wetting the ends of the strips and then pressing them
together to make rings. I managed to do one without getting
my hands dirty, but when the second ring slid open by
mistake, I got glue on my fingers and the paper strip stuck
to them. Waves of panic coursed through my body and
crashed together near my heart. I let out such a ghastly
scream that it shocked me even more than it shocked the
pointy-breasted teacher and the other children. When they
saw the strip of paper dangling from my hand they burst
into laughter.

The woman who had shown the class how to turn stupid
bits of paper into completely useless rings came over to me,
took the strip of paper off my finger and closed my glue
jar. 'Perhaps you'd like to go and explain to Sister why you
don't want to play with clay or glue,' she said in a voice
that made me break out in a cold sweat. She took me to the
class where the nun taught and whispered something into
the folds of her wimple. The nun nodded, took me by the
hand and sat me down in the back desk, behind a girl in a
knitted hat.

The child in front of me smelt so disgusting that I had to
breathe the air inside my own lungs to keep from being
sick. Later I heard that she had sores on her head and had
to have a thick layer of ointment applied to her scalp every
day by the nuns of the Home Nursing Service. The wool
had soaked up the ointment, which had gone rancid, and

.er hat now smelt like a pan of old fat. I began to hate school.

For a week Oma delivered me to kindergarten struggling and crying. When she left I screamed so loud they could hear it in the bakery.

On the Saturday afternoon after my first week of school, my hands came up red and scaly, with blisters under the flakes of dry skin. On Sunday morning, when the garage owner dropped by to drink a gin with Christina and Oma, the blisters began bursting and oozing green pus. Oma wrapped strips of white cloth around my hands but there was so much muck that they were soon saturated. The garage owner loaded me into his old Model T and drove me to the district nurse, who gave me some ointment that smelt as disgusting as my classmate's hat. Once the ointment had been applied, my hands looked even more horrific. The next morning, Oma took one of her home remedies and applied a thick layer to my hands, which she then wrapped in long strips she had torn from old sheets.

She studied me carefully, then started laughing. 'Today, you stay home,' she said.

Although my hands looked normal and rosy again after a week, they didn't take me back to school until I was old enough for primary school, where we were too busy to waste time messing around with clay or glue.

Nine

Whenever Anne dropped in to visit her sisters and tell them about her work at the mayor's, her eyes were gleaming. Martha saw a joy Anne had never known and smiled tenderly.

Martha also saw that the twins were unable to derive any pleasure from their work in the bakery and that they did not share their older sisters' capacity for accepting life as it came to them. Clara hung over the bakery counter with a surly expression and snapped at customers who dared to be fussy. As soon as her work in the shop was finished, she went out for long walks or bicycle rides and did not return home until everyone else was getting ready for bed. She was less moody in the weeks she did deliveries and sometimes talked to customers for hours – deep down she was a sociable chatterbox. Camilla did all her jobs silently and spent her evenings bent over an old sewing machine a widower had given to the sisters – he had been desperate to get it out of his house because he still saw his long-dead wife sitting at it and sewing. At the domestic science school, Camilla had been one of the best pupils in sewing. She didn't need patterns, but just copied any clothes that appealed to her. She made blouses, skirts and dresses in the latest style for herself and her sisters, and my aunts were admired in the village for their fashionable clothing.

The German fashion magazines Camilla sometimes bought included patterns for girl's dresses and these she made for me. There was something funny about them, but it wasn't until I went to primary school that I began to understand what it was. The other girls in the village didn't dress like little German girls and they stared at me as if I had descended from another galaxy. Camilla's clothes were theatrical; they alienated me from the playground.

Since I hadn't been to infant school, I was already behind when it came to making friends. Most of the other girls had the additional advantage of a cousin or neighbour to walk around the playground with, but I didn't know anyone at all and was condemned to sitting on the stone base of the fence and staring out through the green bars, hoping to catch sight of the baker's wagon so that one of my aunts could momentarily wave away my loneliness. I needed a sister who could talk to me during the breaks or help me when someone made snide remarks about my dresses.

Camilla refused to listen when I begged her to make me dresses and pinafores like the ones the other girls wore. She acted as if she hadn't heard me when I told her that no one at school had elbow-length sleeves and asked her to make mine longer as well, and she refused to make dresses with bows, even though all my classmates pulled their dresses tight at the waist with a narrow or wide cotton sash they tied at the back.

I began by protesting weakly, but since no one listened I

soon tried falling into muddy puddles on a daily basis so that my dresses needed constant washing. This campaign had little effect because the washing machine was on every day anyway to get the dirt out of the sisters' pinafores and the bakers' trousers, smocks and aprons – there was always room to throw in a muddy dress as well. Catching it on the sharp corners of the fence proved no better; I was simply given a thrashing for coming home with my second torn skirt in so many days.

For six more weeks I suffered the creations of my pig-headed aunt. Every night I asked God to arrange normal clothes for me, and in the daytime I shuffled along the playground wall and into the classroom, praying that I might melt into the bricks so that nobody could see me.

In my desperation, I began running down everything Camilla made. I knew that it hurt her – she put a lot of love into her dressmaking – but I needed an outlet for my misery. I longed for acceptance and wearing the same clothes could have been a first step towards it.

God finally heard my prayers in two ways. He made Oma spoil a load of washing that included a few of my dresses, and I suddenly had a growth spurt and grew out of the rest of my clothes as well. Christina took me to the boutique next to the church and there we bought skirts, blouses and pinafores just like the ones the other girls wore. They didn't stock anything else. The new clothes made me feel much better, even if they didn't win me a single friend.

Camilla developed the habit of suddenly becoming invisible. Her body would go all glassy, with her bones showing, and if someone opened a window, her skeleton would blow away. I couldn't understand why Martha stood for it. It terrified me, but no one else paid any particular attention.

Martha did however begin worrying that her youngest sisters' youth might wash away in a flood of melancholy and for days she racked her brains for a solution. In the end she suggested that the sisters take turns at finding a job: Clara one year, and Camilla the next. Clara said that she would like to work with a farmer because that would give her a chance to spend a lot of time out of doors. Martha had heard that the tree-nurseryman was looking for someone to help graft and plant out young trees and shrubs.

None of the sisters was better with the cold than Clara. She only started wearing gloves after one of the customers knitted her a pair without fingers, and even then she only wore them in winters when the frost seemed like it would never end and the Meuse was frozen so thick you could cross it in a horse and cart.

Camilla didn't know where to go – until Martha pressed a situations vacant advertisement from a clothing workshop in the city into her hand. Unfortunately, new regulations prevented the workshop from taking girls under sixteen. Because of this, Clara started work first – the laws didn't apply to nurseries – while Camilla continued patiently to sell bread in the shop until she turned sixteen.

On the Monday after her sixteenth birthday, Camilla got onto the city bus at six-thirty in the morning. She was put to work on the production line and given half an hour to sew twenty zips of the same length into the same number of backs of skirts, all of the same colour, so that another seamstress could then join the backs to fronts. She bit down hard on her disappointment and kept it to herself. But in her sleep her sorrow poured out in tears that flowed through the night, so that her sheets and pillowcases needed to be hung out in the sun the following morning. And with puffy eyes she climbed back onto the bus early the next day to sew dozens of zips bravely into dozens of ugly off-the-peg skirts.

The problem was resolved without Martha needing to intervene. The woman in charge of the workshop soon realized that Camilla would never meet her production quota, but rather than firing her, she moved her to the design section, where she made the samples so carefully that they looked like haute couture and the representatives sold more than ever before.

Camilla's move to the design section affected her physically – the bitter lines around her mouth disappeared. She stopped listening to the screaming women she had heard since her birth, and tuned in to songs on the radio instead, songs she could sing along to. She turned out to have a voice that sparkled like crystal.

Ten

A lot of things that were completely normal in other house-holds were mysteries to the sisters. Their mother had died too young to teach most of them how to make jam and preserves, and Martha had forgotten the recipes – she had always been too busy for things like that. Instead, she got Oma to do it for her, and every summer and autumn they bought boxes full of cheap fruit from the local farmers. They used the preserved fruit for their tarts, which had gained a certain fame in the village and surrounding hamlets. Before the old woman came to live with them, Martha had used tins of ready-made tart filling she had bought from a wholesaler in town, but Oma's fruit preserves tasted a thousand times better – her recipes were unequalled.

Oma also had a recipe for a lotion for burns that was based on lilies and salad oil. Several bakers are grateful to this day for her lotion – they were always in a hurry and regularly burnt themselves pulling the glowing hot baking trays out of the oven. Vincentia owed the recovery of her backside to the same lotion.

Although she was very good with the horses, even Vincentia was unable to prevent them from occasionally bolting. The skittish French Canadians in particular would take off for no reason at all, pulling the wagon along behind them. If Vincentia was on the box seat she generally managed to calm the animal down again, but if the horse took off by itself with the wagon in tow, the whole village would join in the fun: everyone wanted to prove how brave they were. Men and boys ran after the wagon or chased it on bicycles, doing anything they could to get the horse to stop. The damage was usually limited, but once the horse took Vincentia completely by surprise and she fell from the box with a foot tangled in the reins.

She was dragged down the street for what felt like a mile. By the time a policeman finally stopped the horse, her overcoat was ripped open, her trousers and knickers were completely worn away and her backside was such a bloody mess that no one dared to look at it.

Vincentia spent three weeks face down in bed with her buttocks covered with oily cloths Oma had soaked in her lotion. Afterwards her derriere was as good as new.

The accident convinced Martha that it was time to deliver the bread with a motor vehicle, something that was now standard in the cities. She asked Christina to invite the garage owner over, and they spent an evening discussing the advantages of a delivery van. There was however one major problem – none of the sisters had a driving licence. Martha saw no point in trying for a licence herself – she didn't want to start taking lessons because she was scared she wouldn't be able to learn the road rules. Marie didn't even answer when they asked her. The conclusion was that

Christina and Vincentia should take driving lessons. The twins were still too young.

Despite the garage owner's efforts, Christina never did manage to pass the test. That is not to say that she never drove the van, but it meant that she wasn't able to deliver the bread by herself. Contrary to everyone's expectations, Vincentia had her licence within a couple of months – she coped with all that horsepower just as easily as she coped with the power of a single horse. Vincentia now had to go out on every bread round, at least until one of the twins had a licence.

Although Vincentia had no great aversion to the work, she still longed for a more varied life. The village wasn't big enough for her fantasies, and she began making weekly visits to the cinema in town, where the Sunday matinée was invariably a cowboy film starring Roy Rogers, Gary Cooper, Gene Autry, Audie Murphy or, later, John Wayne. At the newsagent's she bought postcards of her idols, which she pasted into a scrapbook. On the days she wasn't able to go to the movies, she wrote screenplays of her own, which sometimes included a supporting role for herself. She got so carried away with her stories that eventually she was only capable of falling in love with a man in a hat and cowboy boots, a species not found in the village, or even in town. She was in danger of becoming an old maid, something she did in fact become – but not because she never met the man of her dreams. No, the problem was that, like her, the man in question cherished dreams of his own.

*

The first van was five years old and dark blue. One of the mechanics had spotted it for sale at a bargain price somewhere in Zeeland. Complete newcomers to the car market, the sisters were surprised that it was possible to buy a car for so little. Nonetheless, the amount still exceeded their available funds and Martha needed to arrange a small bank loan. One Sunday morning in early May they set off to pick up the van.

Christina's unofficial fiancé went with them to check whether the van was worth the money, the mechanic went because he knew where to find it, and Vincentia went so that she could practise driving on the way back. Since the garage owner would have to drive his own car back, Christina went to keep him company, and I went along for the ride.

More than anything else, I remember that the trip took for ever. I slept through most of the return journey and only woke up when they were putting me to bed. I heard the story of the trip home from the others, and each time it was repeated more colour was added.

The van seemed a good buy. The engine started at once. There were a few blisters and rust spots in the paintwork, but that was easily fixed, and the owner even knocked some more off the price, so by the time we climbed into the two vehicles to start the long journey home, everyone was grinning broadly: Vincentia behind the wheel of the new van with the mechanic beside her, and Christina and I in the garage owner's old Ford. We followed the van in case Vincentia had any problems.

After just ten miles, the sky went as black as ink and discharged itself in a downpour that scared me so much I lost my voice and was only able to speak in whispers for a whole week afterwards. The drumming of the rain on the car roof sounded like buckets of marbles being emptied out over us. The windscreen wipers were too slow to clear away the water, and visibility got so bad that the garage owner didn't spot the tail lights of the van until it was too late and he had already smashed them with the Ford's bumper. The van had promptly broken down the moment it began to rain.

Christina screamed, the garage owner swore and I opened my mouth without making a sound. We watched Vincentia step out of the van into the pouring rain, assess the damage with a single glance and stride over towards us. She cursed the garage owner so harshly that he almost burst into tears. Christina became so angry with her sister that the two of them got into a terrible row. The mechanic tried to calm the women, but they continued to accuse each other of all kinds of things that had nothing to do with the accident.

Suddenly the mechanic grabbed Vincentia and kissed her full on the mouth – he kept it up so long, I was afraid they would never come unstuck again.

The garage owner started sniggering. He pulled over to the side of the road and got out to look at the broken lights. He had spare bulbs with him, but no red glass. Instead he tore up his red snot-rag and wrapped the pieces around the bulbs. But there wasn't any point in having tail lights unless they could get the motor going again, a job that took well over thirty minutes.

Everyone was soaked to the skin. Then, just when we were ready to leave, it stopped raining and the sky looked as if the weather had been glorious for days.

We drove for almost an hour without any further trouble, then stopped to eat at a roadside restaurant. When we tried to resume our trip home, the van refused to start. Whatever the mechanics did, the engine kept silent so stubbornly that the garage owner uncharacteristically lost his patience. The men decided to attach a long rope to the back of the Model T, tow the defective acquisition to the garage and work out what was wrong with it there.

It took two mechanics almost a month to turn the new purchase into a serviceable baker's van. They had to take the engine apart to get it working again.

They commissioned a carpenter to build wooden racks for the loaves of bread, but when he removed the mat from the rear of the van the floor turned out to be too rusty to take anyone's weight. A new base plate had to be welded in, along with a new supporting beam. Meanwhile angry letters and telephone calls were directed to the previous owner, who refused to refund the extra costs and was equally unwilling to take the wreck back. He simply told them to return it – he would fix it for them.

At last the van was ready. After spending all this time on it, the garage owner and the mechanics decided to respray it. They mixed the paint themselves and came up with a colour that was supposed to be red but was actually midway between purple and pink. Never before had a delivery van had such a peculiar colour. But the sisters loved it.

One of the mechanics painted the sisters' surname on the side in copperplate, with *Bread & Pastries* below it in smaller letters.

The sisters made a real ceremony of the first day of motorized delivery. They decorated the van with ribbons and bows, and gave all their customers a free *knapkoek*, a round flat biscuit sprinkled with sugar that was normally only made at fair time.

The delivery van had another peculiarity: they couldn't lock it properly. The key they had been given only fitted the back door and the ignition. Once again, telephone calls and letters to Zeeland proved futile. Instead, the garage owner made an ingenious construction from two joined pokers. The flat ends of the pokers were attached to the driver's and passenger's doors, thus joining them and making it impossible for anyone to open either door from the outside. After putting this peculiar locking device in place, the driver had to climb over the seat and leave the van through the back, which was nothing if not awkward. It never occurred to anyone to order new keys from the smith.

The van marked the dawn of a new era, but the sisters did not find it easy to give up their horse and wagon – once they were gone, a chapter of the family saga would be closed for ever. The jumpy French Canadian that had dragged Vincentia through the streets had been replaced by the elderly Fritz, a horse that was too slow to bolt unexpectedly and got a wet nose when someone patted him. Fritz was so placid that there were times when even I dared to pat him – he bent down towards me so carefully that I momentarily forgot my fear of horses.

Although no one said as much, we all saw the purchase of the van as a betrayal of Fritz – that was why we didn't sell him together with the wagon. In the summer we put him to pasture in one of our neighbour's fields. Vincentia went out riding occasionally, but Fritz was never in the mood for a spirited gallop and her passion for horse riding soon faded. With nothing left to do, Fritz began to pine: he wasn't used to standing in a field, he was a workhorse, he wanted to hear orders and be told stories about nonsensical matters that were none of a horse's business. When a farmer from the next village to the north came to ask if our horse was for sale, the sisters spent a whole Sunday afternoon debating whether or not to sell. They lubricated the discussion with a whole bottle of gin and decided with moist eyes and full hearts that Fritz was too old to work.

They decided to let the man have Fritz on the condition that he provide him with a happy old age. The farmer promised he would only use him for light jobs and even suggested that the sisters look in on him now and then. No one wanted to go to the field to hand Fritz over, and the farmer said that he could pick him up by himself. That was too much for Christina – she didn't think that was the right way to treat an animal. She cycled to the field and told the horse to go with the man. The animal stared at his mistress reproachfully and refused to go with his new owner, until at last the farmer slapped him hard on the bum and he walked out of the field indignantly.

Their trust in the farmer was misplaced. Instead of keeping his promise, he used the horse he had bought so cheaply for heavy work and didn't even give it enough to eat. Later, when the horse-and-wagon era was almost forgotten in the bakery, Christina and Vincentia bumped into Fritz one last time: emaciated and hitched to a cart that was loaded down with filthy coal waste that was used as a cheap fuel. The animal recognized them and stopped. It was only when Christina saw the reproach in the horse's eyes that she realized it was Fritz. Christina and Vincentia were never able to forget the horse's sadness. Later, they always spoke of Fritz as if he were the only horse they had ever had, whereas of all their horses, he had pulled the baker's wagon for the shortest period.

They had turned the van into a showpiece, but the bonnet concealed a technical drama that developed in various acts.

The first six weeks passed without a splutter. The problems began when Vincentia and Clara used the van to pick up dried fruit from a supplier in the south of the country.

Vincentia did not usually fetch the fruit for the tart fillings herself, but the orders for the summer fair far exceeded those of previous years and the bakers desperately needed new fruit. On the way back from the wholesaler, the engine overheated and cut out. Vincentia called the garage owner, who suggested that she let the engine cool off, top up the water in the radiator, then take it easy the rest of the way home. The sisters gave the engine half an hour to cool off before driving on, but had to stop twice more because the van began to jolt. By the time Vincentia finally steered the van into the village, her hands were clammy with sweat and she promptly declared that she would never again drive 'that bloody thing that bloody far'.

From then on, something was always going wrong. No sooner had one problem been fixed, than the next appeared. The day before the fair and with the van full of tarts, it broke down completely right in front of the church. Vincentia had no choice but to leave it there, where it promptly caused a terrible traffic jam. The garage owner came in his Model T – after first removing the rear seat to make room for the tarts – and drove Vincentia and Clara around to do the deliveries on the outskirts of the village, while Camilla and Anne delivered the orders within the village on foot.

With the onset of winter, the van developed starting problems. It was so hard to start that they often flattened the battery and had to ask the bakers to push-start it.

And these are only samples from the long and pitiful story of a vehicle that was completely indifferent to the sisters' dedication and left a trail of oil and battery acid through their lives. When a connecting rod rammed through the crankcase just before the Feast of Saint Nicholas and sent oil spraying everywhere, including into the cab, the garage owner had had enough. He went to a garage in town, haggled until he had negotiated payment in instalments, and then returned with a shiny red van that did service as a delivery vehicle for five years without a single problem. He sold the purplish-red van's new tyres as partial compensation for his expenses – expenses he never charged to the sisters – and left its amputated shell parked at the back of his garage as an extra storage room.

Eleven

Around the time of all this motorized misery, Anne started coming home more and more often. No one noticed that she had become more talkative. Her sisters were too pre-occupied by their unreliable means of transport to listen to what she was trying to tell them. She did not actually say that she was in love with the mayor – she would not even have been able to put it into words. Anne had always been so sparing with language that she wasn't able to identify the fluttering in her tummy. Only an ear that was open to love's sweet whisperings would have been able to understand her.

If Martha had been paying more attention, she would certainly have intervened before passion sank its roots into Anne's soul. By the time she finally realized what her sister was trying to say, it was too late and she was reduced to the role of remorseful spectator to events that could have been avoided.

As none of her sisters gave the answers she hoped to hear, Anne began visiting fortune-tellers, each of whom told her something different. A woman who specialized in tea leaves assured her that it was only a matter of time before the mayoress was committed and Anne was free to take over the last remaining wifely duties, those in the marital bed.

A famous tarot reader who lived just across the Belgian border laid down his greasy cards and announced that Anne's relationship with her employer would never come to anything. He prophesied that she would spend the rest of her life surrounded by bread and pastries, and advised her to seek redemption with a pilgrimage on foot to the Chapel of Our Lady in the Sand, because the desires she entertained were sinful ones.

Yet another requested a sample of her early-morning urine and smelt it to predict her future. She went back to the fortune-tellers who had given her hope, and once peace of mind had returned to the bakery in the form of a shiny red delivery van, she found willing listeners there as well.

Anne related her visits to the various soothsayers in detail and, together with her sisters, she tore apart the fabric of the different predictions in search of shreds of hope. But the fact remained that the object of her affections was married and his position made divorce unthinkable. The only alternative was to wait for the mayoress to die. Oma said that she knew how to make a potion that would slowly poison her. She had been given the formula by a woman who had used it to murder her husband because he would only make love to her if she disguised herself as a hen with a red handkerchief on her head and two chicken wings on her bum. The sisters all joked about the fatal formula, but none of them dared to take it seriously. Camilla said that she had read about African witch doctors who made voodoo dolls and pierced them with needles or threw them into fires to curse their enemies. She offered to make a doll for Anne to work her magic on. They all laughed heartily, secure in the knowledge that not one of them was brave enough to burden her conscience with the death of the mayoress. For a joke, the baker made a loaf of bread that was the spitting image of the mayoress, and on Saturday evening it was ceremonially cut up, smeared with butter and sprinkled with brown sugar. Sniggering, everyone ate up their slice of mayoress and silently asked God to do something for Anne.

Their prayers were answered sooner than they expected, albeit in a way none of them had quite anticipated.

Just before Christmas, Anne was dismissed by her employer's wife. The woman was sane enough to see that Anne's dedication went too far, and she also saw that her husband's eyes lingered on their housekeeper too often and too long, and that the indifference she herself always encountered in those eyes made way at such times for a look she remembered from the days when they had first met.

The mayor had a guilty conscience and lacked the courage to contradict his wife when she sent Anne packing after an insignificant row over the children.

Anne came home with her tail between her legs and slumped into her father's smoking chair. She didn't shed a single tear and showed no interest in explaining what had happened. One look in her eyes would have been enough to catch the questions she was constantly asking herself, but her sisters avoided her gaze because they knew that they had no answers.

On New Year's Eve the mayor knocked on the door of the bakery looking for Anne. He had had his wife committed that afternoon. The sisters stared at him with astonishment and shared a single thought. No one believed that his wife was mad enough to be locked up, but they were happy for Anne and kept silent.

Martha invited the mayor to celebrate New Year with them. He accepted and partied with the sisters before driving Anne home early in the morning and taking her virginity on the eve of her thirtieth birthday.

The garage owner had discussed marriage with Christina a number of times. He had done it with the clumsiness he brought to everything that was unrelated to motor vehicles.

They first set the date just before Marie's accident, but then postponed the wedding indefinitely because of the concussion and Marie's slow recovery. In the end, the nuptials were temporarily forgotten. The garage owner understood. He had gradually become one of the family and was relatively indifferent to the actual ceremony. He came and went as he pleased and was happy that the sisters had accepted him; in his heart they had long since taken the place of his own family.

Of all the male friends who passed through the house, he was the only one to be given a place of his own, despite being a man who had no experience of women – he had no sisters and the only female he knew well was his sick mother.

Martha was able to get along very well with him too, and this further reinforced the bond between her and Christina. She often asked his advice, and not just on mechanical matters – there were so many things that demanded a male opinion. Martha discussed new business possibilities with him, and he was the one who suggested extending the shop into the hall. After all, it was just a waste of space that earned them nothing and needed mopping every day – and twice a day in rainy weather when people sloshed through in muddy boots. Using the hall would give them enough room for a glass display case for their tarts.

In just one week, the shop was extended while sales continued in the coach house. The new shop was officially opened on the Saturday and fellow shopkeepers sent flowers to congratulate the sisters. Most of the bouquets were made up of hydrangeas – flowers that were big but inexpensive. To this day I still see hydrangeas as flowers with delusions of grandeur. For something so cheap, they are far too sumptuous. They're like streetwalkers trying to play the lady.

While Anne was blooming in her 'secret' relationship with the mayor – a relationship everyone knew about – the garage owner proposed to Christina again. This time they set a date in April. Christina didn't want her wedding to be as grand as Marie's. She was superstitious and thought that all that pomp and circumstance would exhaust your happiness before you even started. Marie's silent return home had strengthened her belief. Christina was careful with her happiness. She knew that she had found a good man, and that he worshipped the ground she walked on, if only in his thoughts. Unwilling to take any risks, she preferred a simple ceremony and a dinner with immediate family. Martha disagreed but respected her sister's wishes. Christina ordered cards from the printer announcing that they *had* married – she planned to send them out afterwards – and early in March she went to town to buy an elegant suit: she didn't even want a wedding dress.

On her way back she stayed on the bus until the last stop in the village, thirty feet from the garage, where she wanted to tell her husband-to-be everything about the package she had left in the shop awaiting alterations. Christina was unfamiliar with the custom that the groom must never see the dress beforehand. She described every line, button and loop of her wedding suit until her fiancé could picture it as perfectly as if she had laid it out before him. He smiled his shy smile. He was sure they were going to be very happy together, and he had never expected anything like this to happen to him. At that moment they heard a choking cough from his mother's bedroom. By the time they got upstairs the sheets and blankets were covered with blood the old woman had coughed up.

In the hospital they sat together by her bedside for two days and two nights until the doctors decided they had done everything their reputations as medical practitioners required and sent all three of them home. They didn't even consider it necessary to arrange for an ambulance. Deathly ill, the old lady had to sit in the back of the old Ford, wrapped in blankets the garage owner had been obliged to go home to pick up first.

Christina spent the entire summer sitting with her prospective mother-in-law and nursing her until finally she
failed to awake from a two-week coma, leaving her son and
his fiancée totally exhausted. No one was in the mood for
a wedding. The bridal suit was wrapped in blue tissue paper,
packed into a box and laid on Marie's linen chest.

Anne too began to entertain fantasies of marriage, even
though she knew it was a virtual impossibility – the mayoress could live for years.

In those first blissful days, everything the mayor gave her
excited her, even the things she was not entitled to. She
shivered when he secretly touched her. She delighted in the
tingling that passed through her skin.

Gradually she began to long for more, she wanted everything a woman has a right to. She started buying sheets and
pillowcases, which she stored away in a varnished linen
chest with copper hinges. Sometimes, when she was back
in her own bed after making love, she slid her hands in
under her nightie and placed them on her tummy. Then she
would breathe in deeply and hold the air tight in her belly,
making it hard and round, and then she would stroke that
firm flesh that softened again when she breathed out. For
just a moment – no longer than a few seconds – she could
imagine bearing a child for the man who had lifted the
sackcloth of loneliness from her shoulders.

She crept into his bed every night. Towards morning she
would return to her own room to sleep – she only needed
a few hours – and wake up in time to get the children up.

The children never saw her in their father's bed. But they

knew and it did not bother them at all – they loved Anne more than they loved their own mother.

It was common knowledge. The village filled with whispering, and the echoes rattled the bakery window. Martha was worried that Anne's happiness might have consequences for their business. She was willing to discuss it with her sister but never quite managed to find the right moment.

The new assistant priest beat her to it. Anne made a ritual of going to confession on the third Saturday of the month to cleanse herself of her sins so that she could climb back into the mayoral bed with an unblemished soul. The Bible forbade it, but the Church gave her an opportunity to redeem herself. In vague terms, she told the new priest that she had transgressed against God's laws. Her former confessor – an elderly priest who had been transferred to a convent where his duties were limited to a daily Mass for the nuns – had never listened to her confession and had never given her more than three Our Fathers for penance. His interest in the sins of his parishioners had waned and died years before.

His successor, however, was still enthusiastic, his vocation fresh in his mind. He listened to Anne's confession and began questioning her. Afraid that her sins would become too great if she lied about them as well, Anne told him exactly what happened in the mayor's home. She was counting on the secrecy of the confessional, but the young priest's conscience was unequal to the burden and, after a week of fretting, he brought the matter up with the parish priest.

The next time Anne returned to the church for her monthly purification at the price of a few Our Fathers, the parish priest stopped her at the door. He had his own standards when it came to matters like forgiveness. He told her that women 'like her', and he spoke the words as if chewing rotten meat, had no right to enter the church. Her sins would be forgiven if she returned to the bakery, because God forgave the worst of sinners if they showed repentance, but she was no longer welcome at the church.

Heart pounding, she returned to the Graeterhof, where she made her lover and employer wait two nights while she fought with the Bible and the desires of her body, which had grown accustomed to the mayor's fleshy fingers. She longed to excite him by drawing flaming stripes down his back with her red-painted nails, she dreamed of wrapping her legs around his arse while he panted, growled and pounded his way to satisfaction. When the forces in her loins had built up enough to block her ears to the priest's voice, she made her way back to the mayor's bed, and this time he snorted and groaned more passionately than ever before.

Anne began going to confession in another village, where she rattled off her sins in an incomprehensible voice for a priest who invariably gave her a penance of six Our Fathers and six Hail Marys. He gave the same to everyone, regardless of the gravity of their sins – he felt that it was up to God to judge.

But finding a new confessional was not enough to safeguard her happiness. One day, at the height of summer, the mayor's lawful wife got out of a taxi late one evening to find her sweat-drenched husband hard at it in the bed where her own conjugal rights had been denied. She swore so loudly the windows rattled in their frames and the whole village would have been able to listen in if the house had been any less remote. It was a mystery how she had managed to leave the asylum. The most likely explanation was that the parish priest had arranged it as revenge.

The mayor was not brave enough to have his wife committed a second time. Anne spent her nights in the servants' quarters and resumed her visits to the card-readers and piss-sniffers. The jealousy of the mayoress reached insane heights and she began tyrannizing the entire household, including the children, who she blamed for not speaking up. She slashed Anne's lace underwear with a big knife, then piled the pink and purple rags on the floor and did a big crap on them. She screamed that she would stick the knife in Anne's fat tits if she dared to creep into her husband's bed one more time. She was no longer able to talk normally – her hatred covered her vocal cords like boils and pus squirted out of her mouth when she spoke. The children were terrified and began going to the bakery after school and staying there until bedtime. They generally ate with Oma, who they now looked on as their own grandmother. The oldest two, who already attended secondary school in town, did their homework at friends' houses and stayed overnight when it got too late for them to cycle back.

Anne had so little to do that she began getting bored and

resorted more and more often to cycling to the bakery to discuss that last shred of hope, which had already been torn out of her hands. None of her sisters had any words of comfort. They avoided her, clearing the way for the stealthy return of her old loneliness.

Now that the nights were her own again, Anne began to use her dreams to rendezvous with her lover. One of the strange women who had peered at her future in a crystal ball had taught her how to lure him into her dreams at night so that they could spend hours walking hand in hand. Sometimes they swam naked in the river until they were too cold and had to return to bed, where Anne woke alone but still able to feel the mayor's hands on her skin.

Six months later, local Gypsy children found the mayoress unconscious in a ditch. The hospital doctors discovered an inoperable brain tumour. Three weeks later she was dead. In sorrow that was painless, tears washed over the coffin, and at the graveside, hypocritical mourners wallowed in feelings that had never existed.

The day after the funeral Anne returned to the bakery. Convinced that the strength of her emotions had summoned Death to the mayoral residence, she no longer dared remain. Now that he was so close by, she was afraid that he might stay and that she might bump into him in one of the long hallways. She went back to sleeping with her sisters and filled her nights with horrible dreams from which she woke shaking. She developed an allergy to lace underwear – the beautiful bras and panty girdles made her breasts and stomach come out in scaly scabs. From now on, she bought her underwear at the boutique in the high street where they only stocked white cotton bloomers and flannel camisoles. She took driving lessons so that she could deliver bread to people she couldn't bear. Her heart had shrivelled to dust and she blew it away when she carried her bridal chest up to the attic.

Twelve

I was already in class one when Anne came back home and put her bridal chest next to Aunt Marie's in the attic. Aunt Marie's chests were locked with keys she kept in the pocket of her slip, but Anne's was not even latched. It was full of things she had collected in the mayor's house: French books she had never been able to read because she had never learned French, scarves of the finest silk, beaded handbags, a strapless green taffeta evening gown she had only worn twice, and a few sets of sheets with lace ruching.

From now on Anne shared a bed with Vincentia and slept between sheets that had been washed with soap flakes instead of modern washing powder. At the table she sat between Oma and Clara.

It was around this time that I first saw the white women.

One night I had to do a pee. I was sleeping between Clara and Camilla because there weren't enough beds now that everyone was back home. My body was wrapped tight in the warmth of my aunts and I wanted to wait for the darkness to thin out, but my bladder kicked me in the stomach like an outraged toddler. I counted to ten very slowly and snuggled up to Clara, whose snoring grabbed my last bit of sleepiness, threw it over its shoulder and carried it away like a grumbling navvy. Now wide awake, I began remonstrating with my bladder, but it refused to negotiate. Finally I wriggled up over the pillows to the head of the bed, then crawled back over the blankets to the foot, where I slid down to the floor. I squeezed my eyes shut and felt under the bed for the chamber pot, but my fingers groped in thin air and found nothing. No pot. I crawled to the other side of the bed, but there was nothing human hands could grasp there either. Someone had forgotten to put the pots back. With my eyes still closed, I pictured them upside down along the side of the courtyard where they had been washed out with bleach, a chore that was unpleasant but essential. I got angry. I didn't care whether it stank of old piss or fresh chlorine, I needed a pot. My bladder needed to eject the grenadine I had drunk out of the glass with the monkey on it while my aunts giggled and guzzled gin. I had no choice but to go to the toilet, down-stairs at the end of the long hall, through the darkness that was as thick as the old sump oil Christina's fiancé stored in big red drums. I had to descend two flights of stairs, go down a cold, black-and-white-tiled hall, then pass through a door that you could never be sure about – there could be long-armed dwarves waiting behind it or anything.

I knelt beside the bed and prayed for courage. When God didn't give me enough after the first prayer, I said another one. Then I crawled to the door, praying all the while that spiders wouldn't run over my hands and scare me to death. My fingers crept up the jamb. They found the door handle, which they very cautiously pulled down, and I crawled through the doorway.

The hall wasn't as dark as I had expected. I could see the stairs so clearly that I could have easily spotted any trolls that might have been trying to hide between the balusters. My first thought was that someone had left the lights on, but on my way back from the toilet, I saw that the front door was open. The light was coming from outside. I hesitated – the night didn't need to be dark to hide enemies – but walked over to close the door. Sitting on the wall of the dairy manager's house on the other side of the street were seven women. They were dressed in white and they waved for me to join them.

I stayed where I was on our doorstep.

'Hello, Emma,' said the woman in the middle. She looked like a larger version of Vincentia. All the women seemed familiar, but they were taller than my mother and my aunts, none of whom was over five foot five.

I walked over to them. They smelt of gin.

'Can't sleep?' asked the woman with Vincentia's face.

'She lost her dreams,' giggled the woman who resembled Clara.

'The door was open,' I said.

'We'll close it soon enough,' said the white Vincentia.

'Why did you open it?' I asked.

'You have to open a door if you want to go out,' said the woman next to Vincentia. 'We'll close it again when it gets light.'

The woman who looked like Camilla grinned and walked into the middle of the street, where she took the arms of an invisible partner and began dancing to music I couldn't hear. She came up to me and asked, 'You coming down to the river?'

'*Now*?' I asked. 'It's the middle of the night.'

'This is the most beautiful time of day, there's music and dancing. Come on,' said Camilla and took me by the hand. I tried to resist but Christina took my other hand and together we all walked to the river, where the light had thousands of colours and there were lots of people in white talking and singing. Everyone was happy and the river I knew so well looked totally different. There was a rainbow and the people in white were dancing under it.

'They look like angels,' I said, 'only without wings.'

'You feel like you have wings here,' laughed Christina.

I saw a woman whose face was covered with a veil. 'That's Truitje,' giggled Camilla. 'For years she's been convinced that the chemist wants to marry her.'

'But he's never asked her,' laughed Clara.

'I don't think he dares,' said Christina pensively.

'He doesn't want her,' said Clara. 'Truitje is too ugly. Why do you think she's wearing that veil?' She ran off laughing.

'Careful!' called Christina, 'you'll fall in the water!'

'She can swim, can't she?' I asked.

'This river is too dangerous to swim in. The water is so warm that you never want to get out again. And you have to be careful of the fish that snap at your soul. If they get their teeth into you, they'll never let go and you'll have to go home without a soul.'

I looked at Christina with astonishment. How was I supposed to know how to look after my soul if I didn't know where to keep it? In my hair ribbons, so that it stuck up on my head like a nimbus, or pinned to the hem of my nightie, so that it dragged along behind me like a train? Suddenly I was terrified.

'I want to go back,' I whispered.

'All right, I'll take you,' said Christina. 'It's not good to come here too often. You could get used to it and then you'd want to come every night. That's dangerous. Sometimes you get lost and end up in the bushes and the long-thorned thistles. They can stick in your heart and get infected.'

Thirteen

Although Anne was back home and helping in the shop, Martha still reminded Camilla about their arrangement. It was Clara's turn to spend a year working outside the bakery and time for Camilla to hand in her resignation. Camilla said that she wanted to wait until spring because there wasn't any work at the nursery in the winter anyway. That sounded logical enough, but when the trees and shrubs began shooting and the nurseryman came to ask when he could count on Clara, Camilla had forgotten her promise. Whenever Martha broached the subject she just shrugged and continued to catch the bus to the city every morning at seven o'clock. She was never back home before six. Every Friday she gave her pay packet to Martha – she never took anything out for herself first, and she never needed to either, because at the start of the week Martha gave each of the sisters pocket money for their personal requirements – and every time Camilla came home with her pay packet, Martha asked her if she had given in her notice. Camilla would shake her head.

'Why not?' Martha would ask over dinner. 'It's not fair to Clara.'

'It's not fair to ask me to do something I don't want to,' answered Camilla.

Martha bit on her lip and glanced unhappily at Clara. 'We can't always do what we want to.'

'Why not?' Camilla asked and promptly left the table to select a piece of material from a pile of remnants she had picked up cheap from the workshop. She wanted to cut out a new blouse.

Martha became nervous. She knew that any solution would involve hurting someone, and that was the very thing she wanted to avoid. In the end, fate lent a hand, which is not to say that the changes it wrought were painless.

These were golden days for the Dutch clothing industry. Fashions were changing ever faster and cheap production countries like Portugal, Morocco and the Far East had yet to be discovered. The workshop that employed Camilla received more and more orders from big department stores with a predilection for double-barrelled names. The boss's eyes sparkled at the sight of his bank statements, which were increasingly enlivened by four-digit deposits. They were the kind of numbers he had once scrawled over his school notebooks to fuel fantasies of wealth. He had never imagined that such amounts might really come his way and he forgot that the money was only partly his. A man of humble birth, he discovered how easy it is to buy status and respect. When the local girls' volleyball team won the national championship, he had uniforms made for them so that they could attend international competitions in style. The club rewarded him by making him a board member.

This entitled him to travel with the team to all major competitions abroad. He invited the entire board to a buffet dinner in his new villa. He bought a sports car. He began a relationship with the model who posed for his brochures and divorced the wife who still wore skirts below the knee.

Meanwhile, the fabric bills were relegated to a drawer he only used for papers he never wanted to see again. The same thing happened to the forms for the income tax and National Insurance contributions. Only the pay packets remained punctual and correct, but that was to conceal the problems from his employees.

From one day to the next, the business went bankrupt. The girls were sent packing and the workshop doors were sealed.

Sobbing, Camilla boarded a bus without checking the destination. She got off again without looking to see where she was and blindly crossed the nearest field.

She was found three days later by a platoon of soldiers on secret manoeuvres. Luckily, one of the men recognized her and the officers arranged for her to be taken home – otherwise she might have spent the rest of her days in an asylum because she was unable to answer the questions the soldiers and their lieutenant put to her. Four days after her disappearance, she sat silently on the wall in front of the dairy manager's house and stared at the house where Caspar lived until Caspar came home from work and asked her to marry him.

*

When it came to Caspar, Martha's solicitousness ricked itself badly. She did not resent Camilla falling in love, but Caspar was hardly a partner she would have chosen for her youngest sister.

Caspar lived a few houses away with his three elder sisters and their club-footed shoemaker father. As if inheriting his father's malformation was not enough, Caspar was also a hunchback. Caspar's sisters never mentioned their brother's deformities; they simply made the necessary allowances and otherwise acted as if there were nothing wrong with him. While he was still going to the boys' primary school on the other side of the village, one of them would always be there to take him or bring him home on the back of her bike, and when it was time for him to start secondary school in town, they had the bicycle repairman make a special three-wheeler with blocks on the right-hand pedal.

At primary school no one had given his deformed body a second thought – he was Caspar the Cobbler and that was all – but as soon as he started secondary school the teasing began. The taunts scorched over his hump and clogged up the chain of his tricycle. He told no one about his tormentors and bravely rode off every day to the city, where he studied so diligently that he had his diploma in just three years with the highest marks ever attained by a pupil of that school, a record that stands to this day. The city council recognized his achievement with a prize, and the local councillor offered him a scholarship to continue his studies, but Caspar took a job as bookkeeper at the brewery and never left the village again – until the day he went to Lourdes in an attempt to regain his health.

*

Caspar was two years older than Camilla. They had played together on the street almost since they could walk. It was Camilla who helped him when the games were too hard for him. She also stuck up for him when someone teased him, something that only happened when children from other neighbourhoods were around.

Caspar was always there in summertime when everyone brought their kitchen chairs out onto the pavement because it was too hot and clammy to stay indoors. People may not have sung as much as before, but they could still spend hours discussing newfangled things like motor cars and television. The women talked about fashion and new materials that dried in next to no time and never needed ironing. Not to mention the phenomenal new undergarment they called the 'petticoat'.

The turning point in Caspar and Camilla's relationship came during the autumn fair when they went on the caterpillar together. For the local teenagers, the caterpillar was the fair's main attraction. It was a palace of dreams, cobbled together from rags and slats of wood and smelling of the sweat of youths on the verge of adulthood who were struggling to master the changes in their glands and bodies. The cubbyholes under the green awnings were niches in a labyrinth of secret desires. They loomed large in the imaginations of the young men and women who spoke of them with blazing cheeks or shy sniggers. The girls stood on the sidelines watching jealously when boys asked other girls to go on the ride with them. Acting on the principle of 'if I can't have it, you won't get it', the boys who didn't have girls jumped laughing into the wagons behind couples so they could whoop and shout out obscene comments and make any forbidden kisses impossible. But nobody got into the wagon behind Caspar and Camilla's – it didn't occur to them that the cripple might have the same desires as young men who were sound of limb.

Unlike the other youths, Caspar did not kiss suddenly and roughly, with closed mouth and drooling lips. Instead he began by telling Camilla that he would like to kiss her, if that was all right by her. She nodded, closed her eyes and turned to face him. Caspar pressed his lips against hers very carefully and a strange shiver ran right down Camilla's back all the way into her white knickers. When she reopened her eyes, he was smiling at her. He bent towards her again, pressed his mouth against hers for a second time and licked the gap between her lips with the tip of his tongue. Camilla pulled away from him with surprise and studied him for a moment before turning away and staring at the curtain that separated the wagons. She climbed out of the caterpillar and walked over to the shooting gallery without saying a word. There, Caspar aimed for a rose but missed because he couldn't rest the butt of the gun properly on his deformed shoulders.

'It doesn't matter,' said Camilla. 'Those roses are stupid anyway. Just get me a cinnamon stick.'

They bought one and shared it, sucking one end each until their lips were close together again, whereupon they burst into laughter and ran over to the dodgems.

*

It was obvious to everyone that Caspar and Camilla's relationship had changed. Night after night they sat together on the wall in front of the dairy manager's house.

Martha asked Camilla why she was seeing so much of Caspar. 'Surely you're not falling in love with that hunchback?' she said and was shocked by the cruelty of her own words.

Camilla looked at her with pain in her eyes and left the house.

Caspar's sisters were no happier with the relationship. They were afraid that their brother would hurt himself. They had always softened the edges of Caspar's world to save him from harm, and now Camilla was there like a giant boulder he could not avoid crashing into. Tormented by visions of him returning home with a lump on his soul as well, they began being mean to Camilla and making spiteful remarks about her, but they lacked the courage to tell Caspar straight to his face that no one in the world could look after him with as much love as they did. They were firmly convinced that only blood ties could allow one to forget the errors of the Creator. None of them had ever been in love themselves and they didn't know how blind love can be. When Caspar announced that he wanted to marry Camilla, his sisters realized that they had not been clear enough.

The next day the three of them went to the bakery to discuss matters with Martha, who had not yet been informed of the wedding plans. There was no question of her giving her approval, not only because of Caspar's handicaps, but also because of the likelihood of their being hereditary.

Martha spent an evening in consultation with Christina and then sent the twins off on holiday with the tour company whose coaches Christina's fiancé still repaired. The twins went to northern Italy, a fashionable holiday destination at the time and the perfect place to meet men.

Clara came back madly in love – not with any special man, but with men in general. She had allowed the coach driver to deflower her at the first stop and had been so astounded by the way the act had made her feel that she resolved to maintain that state of wild ecstasy for the rest of her life. At the Italian border she cashed in this one great love for a vast quantity of smaller denominations and gave herself over to the intoxicating horniness she found in the eyes of waiters, taxi drivers and gendarmes. She would have liked to spend all of her Mediterranean nights with a man, but she was sharing a double bed with her sister and was forced to limit her physical contact with the opposite sex to fumbling in obscure niches or behind jutting boulders on the beach.

The bus driver was so furious that he slept with all the other women on the tour just to make Clara jealous. He even fucked the shrivelled high-school teacher on her first holiday alone, whose moaning and groaning was so loud that it was clearly audible through the whole of their three-storey hotel. Clara didn't notice. She slept deeply every night and was out on the beach at dawn flirting with fishermen, who taught her how to roll freshly caught sardines in sea salt before barbecuing them over charcoal. The accompanying smells became irretrievably linked in her mind with love, and for years she searched in vain for a perfume that smelt of male perspiration and grilled fish.

Rather than diminishing Camilla's love for Caspar, their separation made it all the more intense. She sent him a postcard every day – they all arrived together after she was already back herself, and she was able to read them to him as one long poem.

Martha was furious – her sister could not possibly be happy with a handicapped man. At times she looked as if a thistle had penetrated her heart, and I wondered if she often visited that strange river to forget her troubles.

Fourteen

I sometimes saw the white women around the house. All seven of them were sitting on the attic steps when I got up to go to the toilet early one morning. They looked at me dejectedly. Other times they danced through the hall in the middle of the day singing songs I didn't know in a language I didn't speak. Sometimes they paced the room so nervously they kept me awake; at other times they ran from one room to another slamming doors and panting so heavily that they had no breath left to sing their joyful songs.

I had lost my fear of them, but found it strange that no one talked about them and wondered if anybody else actually saw them.

In the end I brought the subject up with Oma, who told me that they were dreams that wandered at night through unknown regions and remained in our minds as memories of things that had never happened.

I didn't understand. 'But Oma, dreams aren't real, are they?'

'No?' she said and stared at me for a long time. 'When dreams are only illusions, how can you explain feeling so nasty when a bad dream is waking you up?' She shook her head, as if she wanted a quick answer.

'Because it seems so real and you wake up in the grip of fear,' I replied.

'Exactly! That fear stays by you long after the sleep is away. So who can tell you that it is not true what you are doing in your dreams?'

Her explanation didn't really help, but she was right about it often being hard to tell whether you were asleep or awake.

The following night I dreamed that I was going to be kidnapped. In my dream I was being brought up by a woman who was not my mother, and my real mother wanted me back. This was impossible because everyone had forgotten that she was my mother. My mother suggested that she could have me kidnapped and acted out an incomprehensible charade in which a stranger carried me off in a horse-drawn cart. After she had arranged for the police to rescue me, it would be revealed that only she was entitled to bring me up. It was all very confusing and the man who came to get me did everything wrong. A dog he had with him jumped off the cart, dragging a suitcase containing my clothes and toys down with it, but after the cart had driven off, everyone carried on as before, seemingly unconcerned by what had happened until suddenly a lion roared and everyone looked at the back door, because the roar had come from the courtyard, and although I was gone and nobody had got me back, I was still there, and I saw my mother panic completely when the lion came in. She tried to run away, but someone grabbed her and held her tight so that she wouldn't startle the lion, and I wondered how scared I would be if the animal came towards me. I stood my ground. Then I saw that the lion was made of material that had been left out in the rain: a mane of wet cotton thread hung around its fierce face. Then a brass band of animals in disguise marched into the house – it was actually too small for so many people, but everyone seemed to fit – and the stranger with the horse-drawn cart brought up the rear.

That was when I woke up. I spent hours trying to determine whether the events were real or nonsense, but finally made up my mind that the whole thing was nothing more or less than a silly dream.

But once, when I had diarrhoea again and had to go downstairs to the toilet in the hall, I saw the white women in the kitchen. They screamed and stamped around, jostling each other and knocking each other hard against the table. Suddenly they changed into animals. When the woman who looked like Marie turned into a snake and started slithering over the tiles, my arms and legs became as heavy as granite. Martha's doppelgänger became a snarling wolf, and the woman with Camilla's face changed into a big cat that hissed and spat at the wolf.

The wolf started talking like a person, using words I could understand. In drawn-out howls it told the cat that it had to stay with the group, that it wasn't allowed to leave them for others. I saw the woman who looked like Clara grow larger and change colour, until she had turned into a big hairy billy goat, standing on its hind legs and with an enormous penis pointing straight up. The goat roared that hunchbacks can't fuck, and waved its penis back and forth in front of the hissing cat.

I wanted to wake up so that the ghastly images could become memories that I could forget as soon as it got light, but all I could feel was the cold tiles freezing my feet to the bone. I ran up the stairs, forgetting why I had gone down in the first place, and out of protest my rectum emptied itself the moment I crawled back into bed.

My aunts said it was all a bad dream and hushed me. One of them helped me into a clean pair of pyjama bottoms while the other changed the sheets.

My gastrointestinal problems became so serious that our GP decided to send me to a specialist. Christina took me to the hospital in town, where the doctor immediately booked me into the paediatric ward. That was something I hadn't counted on at all, and I was so upset when Christina went off to buy some pyjamas that I started to cry for the first time in years. She came back with a cotton baby-doll set, the first and only pyjamas I ever had with shorts. They were the height of fashion and Christina hoped that they might cheer me up a little. The summer of that year was very hot and the thin cotton was much more comfortable than the flannel pyjamas I was used to, but since then summer pyjamas have always reminded me of an atmosphere of Lysol and camphor.

While the children in the other raised beds were given thin-cut sandwiches and cups of milky tea, a drip was put into my arm. It looked so horrible that it made me cry again, but this time I swallowed my sobs, which bounced around in my stomach as if I had dropped a handful of marbles on the floor. The nurse said that it would all be over soon, and that I would be able to go home again in just a few weeks. She said 'weeks' and it sounded like an eternity. The doctor had said 'for a little while,' and that had been menacing enough. A 'few weeks' meant being closed up for ever in a high cage with white bars.

Visiting hours on the paediatric ward were limited. Just half an hour on Sunday, Tuesday and Thursday afternoons, and those thirty minutes of love were not enough for frightened children like me who had been left behind in a building that was painted the colour of pain. I was unlucky enough to have been brought in on a Thursday and now had to wait until Sunday to see a familiar face. If I had realized, it would have been too much for me to bear. As it was, I spent every minute of the day staring at the ward door until I fell asleep. I hadn't been given anything to eat and my dreams cried out with hunger.

The next morning I was woken up just after dawn. My stomach leapt for joy when a nun put a bowl down on my bedside cabinet, but the sickly smell issuing from it soon brought me back to earth. I turned my head and was confronted by the sight of the other children wolfing down their porridge. I closed my eyes. I hadn't been able to eat dairy products since I was a baby.

The nurse who came around later with a trolley to pick up the cups and bowls was surprised to see that I hadn't touched my porridge. She took a tray, attached it to the bars of my bed and then set the bowl down in front of me. She sat me up and gave me a spoon. I shook my head. 'You have to eat,' she said. 'I'll come and help you in a minute.' After first collecting the dishes and cutlery from the other beds, she returned to mine. She plunged the spoon into the mush, then held it under my nose. I gagged and shook my head once more. Then she held the spoon against my lips, which I kept tightly shut. She smiled nicely and told me that for the time being I wouldn't be getting anything else, not until I was better. I continued to stare at her in hostile silence. She left the spoon in the porridge and studied the chart at the end of my bed. 'You'll have to,' she said, before pushing the trolley with empty bowls and cups out of the ward. I slid down under the tray and tried to go back to sleep.

Halfway down a road that led past big barrels of thick white porridge, I was roughly pulled back to my bed and sat up straight.

'We'll see who's the stubbornest around here,' said a loud voice.

The nun who had put the bowl on my bedside cabinet in the first place was standing next to my bed. She returned the bowl to the cabinet, lowered the side of the bed and gestured to a nurse who was changing the bed of a small girl with long plaits. The nurse came over to my bed and pressed me firmly against the bars at the head of the bed. The nun took a spoonful of porridge, grabbed me by the nose, squeezed it shut and shoved the spoonful of stone-cold porridge into my mouth the moment I opened it to gulp for air. I immediately pushed the back of my tongue up against my palate so that the porridge had no choice but to run down my chin and drip onto my pyjamas. The nun tipped another spoonful of porridge into my mouth but I kept my throat shut even though I needed to breathe and started going red in the face. The nun waited to see how long I could keep it up. My temples began to pound but I didn't give in. The porridge dribbled down my neck and under the collar of my pyjamas.

The nun slammed the spoon back into the bowl so viciously that porridge splashed up into my face. She stamped off in a fury and the young nurse let go of me, after which she asked me as nicely as she could if I wouldn't just eat a little. I shook my head and she too went back to other matters.

At lunchtime the doctor who had told me I had to stay in hospital came by and spoke in whispers with the nun. A little later a nurse I hadn't seen before appeared with a cup of sugar water. Apart from being sweet, it tasted of nothing at all. I drained the cup but hunger continued to gnaw at me, as it would for many days to come.

On Sunday afternoon Martha and Vincentia came to visit. They had a bag of iced biscuits with them and I immediately took two. They put the rest in my locker. As soon as visiting was over, a nurse came and opened the lockers one after the other to collect all the sweets the children had been given. I had the biggest bag of all.

'You don't get it back,' the girl in the next bed explained.

'You have to eat it while your mother's here, then they don't dare take it off you.'

Either way, I never saw any of the sweets again and it was a few days before I had any more visitors.

Usually it was Christina who came. I missed Oma. She hardly ever came because she was too scared to come on the bus by herself and no one else had time to bring her.

The nun made a few more attempts to pour the porridge down my throat but finally gave up. I was given watery concoctions and occasionally half a slice of white bread with a little butter scraped onto it. My stomach screamed so loudly from hunger that it made my eyes water. My bowel movements were runnier than ever.

When Christina came, she read to me from a book she had bought for me and I was briefly able to forget my hunger. Martha only had time on Sundays, and Christina asked if Martha should bring me anything special.

'A chocolate-spread sandwich,' I whispered.

Christina laughed and passed on the request.

Martha arrived with a big shopping bag and pulled out a box of chocolate-coated profiteroles she had baked herself that morning. I hurriedly jammed one into my mouth and was immediately given a second, which I also gulped down, albeit a little more slowly than the first.

Martha didn't have much to say. She gave me a colouring book and pencils and said that Oma had been moody lately. I promised to draw a picture for her and took a third cake. Five minutes before visiting was over, Martha got up to go. She left the two remaining profiteroles behind in my locker, hidden under a pair of pyjamas, because I had told her about the sisters taking everything away.

Watching Martha walk out through the ward door, I felt very strange. An overwhelming desire to go home to the house that smelt of freshly baked bread rose up within me, and all of a sudden my stomach emptied itself all over my sheets.

The girl in the next bed started to scream: 'She's throwing up blood!'

The ward sister ran up to me in a panic and immediately drew the curtains around my bed. A little later she returned with the nun, who slammed down the left-side panel of my white cage and roughly plonked me down on the chair, which Martha had forgotten to slide back under the bed. She looked questioningly at the nurse who was mopping up the worst of the mess with a cloth. 'Chocolate,' she whispered, pulling the sheets off the bed. The nun pulled everything out of my locker and studied the profiteroles with disgust.

I was roughly helped into another pair of pyjamas and put back into bed with the sheet tucked so tight under the mattress that I wouldn't have been able to move even if I had dared to try. I chewed on the sour taste in my mouth and dozed, but woke up when they wheeled my bed out of the ward. I wasn't given a chance to say goodbye to the other girls.

My bed stopped with a jolt in a high-ceilinged room with glass walls. White curtains were hung up at eye level to stop me from seeing the children in the other cubicles. The door was locked with a key the sisters kept on a cord around their waist. Whenever someone wanted to come in, they used the key to unlock the door. Everyone had one, even the nurse who came to put in a new drip and the pale woman who took my temperature. And they all locked my glass cubicle behind them. This was one of the 'boxes' the other girls had talked about with ice on their tongues. Here even Christina wasn't allowed to come to read me her stories.

Unable to sleep, I listened for the chapel bell. It rang every quarter of an hour, and every quarter of an hour I counted the number of times it rang. I wondered how long it would take before I was old enough to die.

The next day Christina appeared at the door. I thought she had come to comfort me. She said something, but I couldn't understand because the door was shut and her words were muffled by the thick glass. I shrugged my shoulders. And I saw that her sorrow was too great for the misery I was being subjected to.

For minutes she stood there staring blindly in my direction. She began to whisper to a nurse who nodded and pulled out the magical key on a cord. The sister opened the door and let Christina in.

She pulled a chair over to the side of my bed.

'Jannes has gone into hospital,' she said after a while. 'They say it's not serious.' She was quiet and looked at the window, as if she might catch sight of him over in the other wing where the men's wards were.

'What's he got?' I asked.

'They're not sure.'

'Then how do they know it's not serious?'

She looked at me. 'That's what I'd like to know. I think they're talking through their hats.'

Christina had married her garage owner just two months earlier in a quiet ceremony. No one had been present except for Martha and an uncle and aunt of the garage owner. After a simple dinner in town, they had gone off on a three-day honeymoon to the Ardennes. On their return, Christina had moved into the house next to the garage, where she slept with her husband in the bed that had belonged to his ailing mother and which still gave off a lingering air of disease.

Since getting married, Christina had visited home so regularly that no one had felt as if anything had changed. She still helped in the bakery and the shop, and on Sunday afternoon Martha and I often dropped by at her place for tart and coffee. But that was something we had done before her marriage to the garage owner as well. The only difference was that Christina no longer went home with us for the night.

Christina's husband was seriously ill. He had a growth in his lungs – possibly caused by poisonous fumes in the poorly ventilated garage – and none of the doctors expected him to live long, even though they were constantly telling my aunt that he would soon be able to go home.

Christina visited him daily. She came to see me in my glass cell as well, and if the bad-tempered nun wasn't around, the nurses would let her in so that she could talk to me for a few minutes or read a story from the book she had given me.

Sometimes she got lost in the stories, and if she noticed that she had wandered off on unknown paths, she would smile sadly. 'I think I was too careful with my happiness,' she said. 'I had a beautiful cake in front of me and now the cream has gone sour.'

I looked at my aunt and could taste how bitter her happiness had become.

At night I cried for her, and without my realizing it, her sadness became intertwined with my own. When my heart had grown so hard that it no longer existed, I suddenly heard music, so soft that my heart had no choice but to relax to listen to it.

At first the sound seemed to be coming from far away, but then I realized that it came from within my own cell. It was the sound of a mouth organ, forming the melody of my sadness, and after I had listened to it for long enough, my tears dried and I fell asleep. I dreamed of Jannes, who was better again and smiling his shy smile. He walked up to someone who shook his hand and led him away.

The next day they took me back to the ward.

After seven weeks I was allowed home. One afternoon Vincentia arrived to pick me up in the delivery van. She told me that Jannes had been buried the day before.

Christina continued to live in the house next to the garage but came to the bakery more and more often. On Saturdays and Sundays she was there all day. She kept the garage going to avoid putting the mechanics out of a job, but she knew nothing about cars and had no idea how much to charge for repairs and spare parts.

She advertised the garage three times in the regional newspaper, but instead of a buyer, Jannes's brother arrived demanding his share of his mother's estate. He paid Christina next to nothing. He wanted the garage all for himself, but neglected the business so badly that it went bankrupt in just six months. The garage and house were sold together. Christina had gone back to sleeping in the baker's house long before.

Fifteen

I came home to a changed house. At first I thought it was because of Jannes, but gradually I realized that something else had happened during my long stay in hospital. Vincentia and Martha were hardly speaking to each other, and when they were forced to say something, Vincentia's words blurred into a snarl.

Vincentia should have been a boy. She was built like a block of cement and had a voice that was made for swearing. Alone among the seven sisters, she had uneven, pock-marked skin, the result of a brief but intense bout of acne. When she was almost sixteen, a horde of bright red pimples with white heads had appeared on her face. After being squeezed and treated with Oma's ointments, they had left deep craters and permanent scars.

Vincentia had not worn a skirt since she was seventeen. The only feminine thing about her was her mania for reading, but unlike her sisters and friends, she never identi-fied with the female characters in the books she read. She followed the men in the stories, jumping up onto the backs of their horses and riding off with them, sometimes going so far from home that her sisters had difficulty getting her back again.

One day a farmer gave her the use of a piece of land on the edge of the village, close to the forests and the German border. She borrowed implements from the farmer and harrowed and ploughed the earth. She sowed maize and went there every evening after work to watch the plants inching upwards out of the soil to gradually form a green forest she could walk through with an elated expression, from north to south and from east to west, down every row, stroking all her plants. Finally she came home excitedly with her first ear of maize, far from ripe, which she then hung above her bed and left there for years, until all the colour had faded out of it. The harvest of that first year failed – the ears went mouldy – but early next spring she began anew with undiminished enthusiasm.

During my stay in hospital she began going to the cinema more and more often. She had met a man there who wore a cowboy hat: an authentic Stetson, 'Made in Missouri'. His boots might not have had fancy stitching or slanted heels, but they were made of rough unpolished leather. He only knew a few words of Dutch, but she was doing a correspondence course in English and that, together with the few words she had picked up from all those Westerns, enabled her to more or less understand him.

Her new friend told her about 'the States', and the mere fact that he never bothered to call it America was enough to give her goose flesh. Their conversations transported her to a far better world. With few words but lots of love, they discussed the prairie, mustangs, ranches and herds of cattle that needed to be rounded up and driven to the horizon. Together they made plans to travel to the States, and the sooner the better. But first, she had to be patient: he was in Holland because his uncle was dying. He had made a solemn promise to look after him and arrange the funeral when the time came.

Physical infatuation and her love for an illusion became entangled in Vincentia's mind. Her cowboy kissed her when they danced, but that wasn't something she particularly liked. Men's kisses had never loomed large in her dreams. She was much more excited by the fact that she was the one he had chosen to take back to the US of A. When he pulled her into a dark corner on the way home and tried to undo her shirt and paw her breasts, she shoved him aside and was upset for days.

The other sisters teased her about her eccentric romance, but their jokes were so innocent that even Vincentia laughed. Martha was unable to believe that Vincentia might really leave – America was so far away that she couldn't even imagine it. She made some casual enquiries about the man's family and his sick uncle, but no one seemed to know them.

Then she found out by a fluke that Vincentia's Yank was an ordinary Limburger who had grown up in a nearby hamlet with a reputation for keeping its back turned to the outside world. The young man who claimed to have been able to ride a horse before he could hold his head up straight was actually the son of one of the bakery's most faithful customers. The sisters didn't know him or his family because his mother always bought her bread in the shop. For some inexplicable reason, none of them had ever met him at the dance hall either, although he must have been there often enough – he was an outstanding dancer. By pure coincidence, another customer started talking about Vincentia's obsession with cowboy movies while the young man's mother was in the shop. She explained that her son had a similar fascination for everything that smelt of horse sweat and boot leather. 'If it was up to him, he'd leave for the Wild West tomorrow,' she laughed, 'but fortunately he doesn't know the first thing about farming, and clerks who don't speak English aren't in demand over there.'

Seeing that Vincentia was at risk of drowning in the river of her dreams, Martha bore the burden of her knowledge for three whole days before deciding that it was her responsibility to pull her sister up onto the bank. She tried to play it down by relating her discovery over dinner as if it were a great joke.

Vincentia stiffened. Her face went as grey as Oma's hair. 'It's not true,' she whispered. 'You're talking about someone else.'

Martha passed the truth across the table, and Vincentia silently mashed it into her potatoes. Then she stood up and left the room and the house to wander aimlessly over the heath.

For hours she shuffled along paths she had once ridden down while fantasizing about open plains. She didn't come home until the moon had completed half of its circuit of the heavens, and then she went straight to bed without saying a word.

She stopped going to the cinema in town and dumped the scrapbooks with photos of film stars in a corner of the attic. Although she no longer used Sebastian's saddle, she had never let a week go by without cleaning and waxing it – now she left it to dry out and crack. With her dreams shattered, she was forced to live in an unbearable reality. The lump in her throat was so enormous that no words could get past it.

Vincentia's romance had taken place beyond my field of vision – by the time I came home from hospital it was all over. Another thing I missed was the start of Martha's new relationship. The dried-fruit wholesaler had fallen in love with Martha on a Sunday when he personally arrived with an express delivery to replace five bags of prunes that had been infested by a horde of weevils and were needed to bake twenty-five tarts for a wedding on the following Tuesday. Invited into the kitchen for a coffee, the wholesaler settled down at the table and seemed in no hurry to leave. When he was still sitting there after his third cup, the sisters offered him a gin to wash it down, and then another, and since they were all drinking too, they got a little giggly and started cracking jokes and making fun of each other. The wholesaler was a childless widower who had lived alone for years. He was very sensitive to the warmth around the stove in the sisters' kitchen.

After that first evening, he often brought their orders himself, even though he had no shortage of staff. And he almost always stayed to drink a coffee in the kitchen with Martha and Oma. Martha didn't notice a thing – her senses did not respond to men who fantasized about running their hands over the curves of her body – but once her sisters began commenting, she was forced to face up to something she had been ignoring since the day Sebastian abandoned the bakery. She tried to resist, but no matter how much she busied herself with pointless tasks when he was around, she could not keep from blushing every time he spoke to her.

After Oma had broken the ice by inviting him to dinner on the Sunday of the summer fair, he took the initiative and made his Sunday visits a fixed event. He was nice to the other sisters. He often brought presents for them and he always brought something for me. The first present he gave me was a game of skill, a round box with a glass lid. Inside the box was a metal mouse you had to manoeuvre into a cage. It was easy but fun, and perfect for moments when time was in no hurry to get anywhere.

The man proposed three times before Martha broached the subject with Christina. She had always rejected a second marriage as impossible. Sebastian had been gone for almost ten years and could have been dead for all they knew, but Martha was still married to him. Now she took advantage of Christina's increasingly frequent visits to the bakery to tell her about the marriage proposal and her doubts. Christina listened, then took her older sister by the arm and led her past all the beautiful moments they had seen passing by in the distance. Weaving a story from other peoples' memories, she was suddenly overcome by an intense sorrow about the life she hadn't lived. She reminded Martha that a woman's path in life leads to a man's bed and that life is empty if you always have to sleep alone.

Martha was unsure and wondered how she could combine marriage with her work in the bakery. She decided to talk about it with everyone on a Saturday evening and bought two bottles of gin just to be on the safe side. Perhaps it was wrong of her to wait until the first bottle was empty before laying her cards on the table. Perhaps it was the wrong moment, perhaps she chose the wrong words. She said that she could easily combine the two things, that she would continue to arrange everything and that no one need worry, nothing would change.

It was as if she had smashed the bottle of gin against the stove. Suddenly emotions were ablaze.

Using all the words she had kept to herself for weeks, Vincentia hurled her shattered dreams against the wall of the kitchen. She screamed that she would be glad to see Martha leave for ever so that she wouldn't be around to uncover any more nasty secrets she could have found out for herself without being made a fool of in front of the whole family. 'You can't keep your nose out of anything, you take over everything!' she screeched.

Martha looked to the others for help. She didn't know how to deal with reproaches.

Marie chewed on her gin and nodded. 'It's true,' she said. 'You never let us do anything ourselves. If you hadn't been so pushy, I wouldn't be married yet. You made me rush into it before I was ready.'

'When *did* you want to do it? When you were all dried up?' asked Martha.

'I might never have got married at all! But at least it would have been my decision,' said Marie.

'Mama made me promise to look after you all,' Martha said, sobbing. 'That's all I ever did. I've spent every day of my life on you.' She cried the tears her mother should have been there to wipe away. She cried because she would rather have been a sister to the six girls she had been forced to care for as if they were her daughters. She cried because her father had chosen not to help her. Maybe she also cried about the man who left because he was unable to help her. And she cried because she so desperately wanted to hear that she was irreplaceable, and no one said it. She felt more useless than stale bread – at least that was still good enough for pigs.

'We're old enough to look after ourselves,' said Camilla. 'If Mama was still here, she wouldn't have forbidden me from seeing Caspar. You think you know everything, you want to be better than Mama.'

'Stop calling her Mama! You never even knew her,' snapped Clara.

And these were the words that moved Camilla to tears. 'It's not my fault Mama died because of me. If I'm to blame, then so are you. You killed her just as much as I did,' she sobbed.

'What are we doing?' lamented Christina. 'No one killed Mama.'

'Yes they did, it was Father's fault! He should have kept his hands off her,' exclaimed Marie. 'He should have left her alone, we had enough children. Men only think of themselves. They've got one-track minds. If they can't have their way with that thing of theirs, then a woman's no good. They're disgusting!'

Everyone looked at her in astonishment.

Clara started giggling, Camilla cried that she didn't know what Marie was talking about, and Christina whispered that going to bed with a man could be lovely and started crying, thinking about those few nights with Jannes, who had made love to her so tenderly that the sheets were still clean the morning after he took her virginity. Her breasts felt those big hands that had left the smell of oil on her nipples, a smell that still rose up from her blouse in warm weather. Anne looked at Christina and recognized true love, and she too opened the floodgates to the tears she had been holding back since leaving the mayor.

The evening ended with them all bawling, and the next day their eyes were red and swollen and the washing machine was full of tear-stained handkerchiefs.

After lunch, which was eaten in silence, the dried-fruit wholesaler arrived in his car. Martha got in without a word. She was carrying a single suitcase containing her clothes and a few small possessions, things like a statue of Mary she had bought from the carpenter, who did woodcarving in his spare time. Otherwise she didn't own a thing in the whole house. She didn't have any embroidered sheets because she had never had time for embroidery, and she didn't have any sheets with lace ruching because she had never helped herself to the contents of the till.

Sixteen

We didn't hear from Martha for a month. Not until her
fiancé came to invite us to the wedding. Martha's prospective
husband was well connected and his influential friends had
found a way to dissolve her previous marriage quickly.

Martha would have preferred a quiet wedding, but her
fiancé's family were determined to make a big party of it.
They wanted music, singing and dancing. Since she was in
a new foreign environment where other people made the
decisions, Martha let them have their way.

Christina and I were the only members of the family to go
to the reception – the other sisters cuddled closer to their
resentment. Marie gave us one of her unused sets of sheets,
wrapped in silver paper. Anne dumped her luxurious lingerie
onto the table with the words, 'Maybe she can use these,
'cause I'm scared that fellow will run for it if he sees her in
those patched knickers of hers.'

Christina left the frivolous underwear behind, but sent
me out to buy a silver candlestick, which she wrapped up
and decorated with a big red bow.

*

I was impressed by the sight of Martha entering the church. Although the Church did not officially recognize the marriage, the priest had proved willing to say a Mass – without blessing their union. Martha wore a pearl gown that fell beautifully over her narrow hips. A generous satin sash was tied in a bow at the back to camouflage her shortcomings in the bottom department. The neckline was cut low to reveal a voluptuous cleavage, her breasts having been squeezed into her first ever deluxe push-up bra. The hairdresser had put up her long chestnut hair and pinned white flowers into the roll. The woman before me was a stranger, someone who couldn't possibly be 'Mother'.

Martha's husband had asked her if she wanted to have me with her. She asked me on her wedding day, but I knew it would mean changing schools and having to make new friends – something that was surely beyond me – and that I would be given a room of my own – an unpleasant prospect because the only time I had ever slept alone had been in hospital. I asked her if Oma and my aunts would stop talking to me as well if I moved in with her, and she said she didn't know. I told her that I couldn't bear that.

I partied as if I had nothing to do with her and tried to hide the embarrassment I felt when everyone turned around to look at her when she danced.

It was an impressive wedding, but it had nowhere near the feeling of togetherness of Marie's. Neighbours and business associates had only been invited to the reception – a custom that was just coming into fashion – and that put an end to the usual spontaneous serenades. The groom's brothers-in-law and cousins had rehearsed a risqué ditty and two nieces recited bland poems during the meal that followed the Mass. A professional band played songs from before the war but no one sang along – they couldn't remember the lyrics.

The newly-weds went for three days to Brussels, where Martha's husband needed to meet with a tropical-fruit importer. Afterwards they returned to his home city.

I only visited them once – on Martha's next birthday. Never again. She never came back to help during busy periods either. On rare occasions she talked to Christina over the phone, because Christina had moved back to the bakery and resumed doing all the things she had once done with Martha. Surprisingly little changed in the rhythm of our days.

I didn't see my mother again until Sebastian died three years later.

When Christina and I returned from the wedding it was cold in the house. Marie's silence became so total that we began tiptoeing around. Vincentia's anger had won itself a permanent place at the table. Camilla was hearing screaming women again. Anne suddenly began to eat vast amounts. She ate all the things that normally went into the slop bucket for the neighbours' pigs. She swelled up into a formless lump of flesh, the fat accumulating like the rings of a tree: if we had sliced her open later, we would have been able to count her years of bulimia, with her former firm body at the core. She had become so terrified of attracting desirous male glances that she couldn't stop stuffing herself. She bloated and became a thing that everyone turned away from in horror, and Camilla had to make sack dresses for her from pieces of material as big as sheets.

Camilla whipped these dresses up quickly, whereas she devoted more and more time to the wedding dresses she was asked to make for girls who were free to marry their love. Martha's departure had only increased the difficulty of marrying Caspar. Camilla was unable to marry because her father had disappeared and could not give his permission. The law stipulated that to marry, women under the age of thirty-one needed the signature of their parents or of a guardian, and an official guardian had never been appointed.

Now that Martha was older and a married woman, a lenient attitude on the part of the authorities would have allowed her to be appointed Camilla's guardian, but the situation was unclear and Camilla was too stubborn to ask Martha to help. Instead, she spent hours in her garret making wedding dresses she would have liked to wear herself. She tried on each dress as it was finished and called Christina to come and take photos for the scrapbook she kept. Later she would show the photos to Caspar and once again ask him what he would like to be wearing when they met at the altar. They then spent hours discussing the wedding they were both looking forward to so keenly.

Seventeen

After Martha moved out, the house died.

Two months after her elder sister's wedding, Marie left the house for a convent in the south of the country. Once a month she wrote a letter describing in a few words her life in the convent, where she was put to work in the kitchen and had no time for embroidery.

She never took up the annual leave that would have allowed her to visit her family. She didn't come back until Sebastian's funeral, and then she shed her habit for good.

Soon after Marie entered the convent, Anne found a position in town as twenty-four-hour help for a blind man, who had no objection to her outsized body. The job did require her to overcome her aversion to physical contact, as she was unable to avoid touching him when handing him things. The man also wanted to go out for occasional walks during which he held on tightly to her arm. Although it was hard for her to adjust to these things, she was able to get along well with the man.

After announcing several times that she didn't want to stay working in the bakery, Clara disappeared literally from one day to the next. She didn't contact us, and for three years we had no idea where she was. When she finally came back, she didn't explain where she had been or what she had been doing all that time. It was only when her children were dumped on our doorstep that we realized she had run off with a man.

Camilla got a job with a bridal boutique in town, where she altered wedding dresses that were too long, too loose or too tight, and designed matching dresses for the bridesmaids and flower girls. Without consulting any of us, she moved into the empty flat above the shop. We only saw her when she walked down the street with Caspar, who never visited her in town.

Vincentia still slept at home, but now spent all of her free time with the cabinetmaker, who was teaching her woodwork. She did the bread round alone, something she could easily manage because she no longer chatted with the customers, who complained to Christina but did not change bakers because, as luck would have it, the other baker was even less of a gossip.

Christina hired a second journeyman baker to meet the increasing demand for pastries and cakes, and also began selling more and more products on the side – starting with coffee, tea and sugar, and ending up with things like mops and washing powder as well.

Now and then Christina had me do little jobs like running errands or washing the windows and mopping out the shop, but Oma still did everything she possibly could for me. I adopted my aunts' addiction to reading and spent every spare minute hidden away somewhere in the house with my stories. The school library received five new books each month and the head nun, who was also the librarian, always gave them to me first because I had already read all the old books.

When the group of strangers carried Sebastian in and laid him on the living-room table, almost three summers had passed without Martha. I had finished primary school and was due to move on to the domestic science school in September – it was still run by Sister Redemptora, who by this time smelt of mothballs.

Anne was back home. About eighteen months after she had begun looking after him, the blind man had died, leaving her his savings of some twenty thousand guilders. She used the money to buy a second-hand Porsche, but she was too fat and couldn't fit into it, so after a week she took the expensive sports car back to the dealer and exchanged it for a brand-new Volkswagen that was a little more roomy and had a driver's seat you could slide back. Every Sunday she used her new car to take us to places we had never been before. She began with nearby cities – Maastricht, Liège and Aachen – but wanted to go further and further, sometimes deep into the German Eifel, so that we often didn't get home until late. Oma had a low tolerance for sightseeing, and she would usually doze off on the back seat and be snoring loudly even before we had left the village.

Camilla came back that same summer, because the owner of the boutique had begun harassing her in the upstairs flat. When he tried brushing up against her in the shop as well she told him to go to hell and started making her own wedding dresses at home. She also altered the off-the-peg clothing in the village's only boutique.

She was now able to spend as much time with Caspar as she liked. He came to dinner more and more often, and after the meals he taught me arithmetic – thanks to his infinite patience it ended up being the only subject I ever got high marks for.

Clara was suddenly back again as well, without a word – the sisters all had the habit of clapping a hand over their mouths whenever their hearts tried to speak. Clara went back to sharing the bread round with Vincentia and helped clean and grease the baking trays as well, so that Christina had no choice but to dismiss one of the bakers.

With the exception of Martha and Marie, everyone was back home when Sebastian was carried in.

Eighteen

The day after Sebastian's funeral Oma told me that she had seen a woman in white in the hall. The white lady had told her to come with her. Oma didn't know the woman, who had refused to say where they were supposed to be going.

A week later, on Saturday, just before dinner, she came running out of the kitchen. 'She was wanting to drag me away! She was saying things would be good for me there and that I looked after you long enough already.' With a frantic look in her eyes, Oma shouted, 'But I want to stay many more years with all of you and looking after Emma!'

Christina grabbed her, pushed her back into the kitchen and sat her down in Grandpa's armchair.

Martha poured a gin for her. 'Oma,' said Martha, 'you can stay with us as long as you like, but if you don't want to keep on working, just say so. If you're too tired, you don't have to do a thing.'

But Oma wasn't tired, she was confused. More and more often her eyes gazed straight through walls and doors, and she no longer dared to admit to all the things she saw there, although she would have been so happy to look at them together with us. She had never felt so alone.

*

A couple of weeks after Sebastian's funeral – I was in the kitchen with Oma, who was knitting socks while I did my homework – she said, 'There is always more.'

'More of what, Oma?'

'Of them there!' she said. 'There is always more of them and always waving.'

'But where?' I asked.

'Look there, there by the stove,' said Oma. 'Waving, always waving. Don't you hear them calling me?'

There was a pan of potatoes on the big stove in the corner of the kitchen, near the window. There were ten small sausages in the frying pan, and we were warming up some spinach in another saucepan. The lids were rattling because no one had put them up on the edges of the pans.

'Oma, who can you see? Do you know them?' I asked.

'No!' said Oma angrily. 'I never seen them before, but every time they come back. When I go to the toilet, they stand in the hall. When I lie in the bed, they sit by the window. I don't want to talk with them, I'd rather be telling you a story.'

'What do they tell you, Oma?'

I didn't know what to say. I couldn't see anyone next to the stove. I didn't bump into anyone in the hall either. I hadn't seen my white women for ages, and I wondered if Oma was seeing them now.

When she had to go to the toilet, she would get nervous and pull me along behind her. She would leave the door open, something none of us did – after all, it was the only room in the house where you could be alone. I stared into space in the empty hallway while listening to Oma's pee splashing into the toilet bowl. I was ashamed to have to share something so intimate.

But Oma was no longer concerned about such things. Standing there, pulling up her knickers, she would ask, 'They still there?'

I reassured her and led her back to the kitchen, where she knitted faster than ever and hardly looked up from her work. She whispered stories into the wool and dropped more and more stitches. Her knitting never again achieved the shape of a sock.

In the middle of the third week after Sebastian's funeral, Oma started avoiding the kitchen. She bustled around her room all morning – one of us went up to check on her now and then – and when we called her down for lunch she cut through the coach house – which had been called the garage ever since we bought our first van – and sat down in the courtyard. She said that she wasn't hungry. Martha asked me to take a plate of food out to her and to stay there until she had eaten it.

Absent-mindedly Oma jabbed her fork into her potatoes and ate a piece or two of the meat Martha had cut up for her.

'Oma, if you're tired you should have a nap in Grandpa's chair this afternoon,' I said.

She looked at me fearfully and said that she didn't want to go back into the kitchen. I promised to stay with her, but she continued to refuse and never set foot in the kitchen again.

'I am going to lie down on the bed a while,' Oma said,

with her plate still full of meat and potatoes that had now grown cold.

In the evening she wanted to go out walking with me. Martha thought it was too tiring and told us to sit in the courtyard instead, but Christina pushed the two of us out the door and told us to walk around the block a couple of times. Oma headed straight for the church, but in those days they had already started locking it late in the afternoon and we couldn't get in.

Oma was upset for a moment – she was obviously planning something – but recovered and said, 'Then we go to the chapel.'

She pulled me along with a strength I no longer expected, and we walked at a brisk pace to the edge of the village, where the roadsides were raggedy because there were no gutters or pavements to keep them straight. At the end of these back roads were two rows of cottages and a small chapel that was always open for the people from the cottages, who found the church in the village too far away for their contact with God.

Oma sank to her knees in the front pew, clasped her hands in prayer and said three Litanies of the Saints, after which she wanted to say a whole Rosary with me. Her prayers were so intense that they scared me, and I did what she asked. Afterwards she left the chapel with a sigh of relief, and led the way back to the village, again walking as fast as she could, and pointing out things along the way and insisting that they were all so beautiful.

*

When we got home Martha slapped me hard – for the first time in my life. My aunts were furious at me, and I was sent to bed, even though it was still light out. The next day Oma was still asleep when I came home from school in the mid-afternoon, and she didn't wake up at all that day or night. I knew that Oma was arguing with the white people in her sleep and the next day I insisted on staying home from school so I could hold her hand tight. Now and then shudders passed through her body, and she growled fiercely. At the end of the afternoon she quietened down and opened her eyes. She smiled and looked at me with satisfaction, closed her eyes and fell asleep again. When I hugged her she was burning hot.

Christina came and saw me with Oma in my arms. 'Oh my God, she's passed away already,' she said. 'That didn't take long. I'll phone Sister Cyrilla.'

I laid Oma back on her pillow, looked at her face, which was slowly changing, and then back at Christina. I had no experience of death and hadn't seen what Christina had seen. I tried to imagine that the woman in the bed was now dead, even though she was still very warm and had a calm sleepy smile on her lips. One after the other, the sisters came and hugged her. I stayed sitting by her and touched her every now and then until the district nurse arrived. I felt the warmth gradually leave her body.

'How peaceful she looks,' said Anne.

'It's a blessing that she didn't suffer,' said Vincentia.

*

When I went back into Oma's room the next day, she was gone. On the bed lay a woman of light-blue wax.

Oma was buried on Saturday afternoon, too soon according to the Church, but Martha didn't want a dead body in the house on a Sunday – she believed in the saying that dead people laid out on Sundays tend to draw family members along in their wake. 'A corpse on a Sunday keeps the church-yard busy,' the old people said, and we'd had enough deaths for the time being.

Martha ordered a headstone of Italian marble but we didn't know what to put on it. We didn't know Oma's date of birth or even her name – there were no papers among her possessions and she had never registered at the town hall. All we knew was that we missed her, so that was what we had carved on the stone.

Losing Oma left me with just half a heart. Searching for a way to make it whole again, I began talking to Martha.

Nineteen

After Sebastian's funeral Martha had stayed on at the bakery. No one asked her when she would be going home and no one brought up the subject of her abrupt departure. It was as if the three years of her absence had not existed. Vincentia spoke to her normally and Christina discussed business matters with her, just as she always had. When her husband rang up to ask whether he should come to pick her up, Martha answered 'soon', but after Oma died this period was extended and everyone understood. Her husband came to Oma's funeral and went home alone – just as he had after Sebastian's funeral.

Martha sat down at her old spot at the table, played cards and ludo with us and laughed loudly with Christina at Clara's and Vincentia's jokes.

At first there was not much talk of the past, even though this was the perfect opportunity to go over it all again. In the pockets of Sebastian's tattered clothes the sisters had found images they had forgotten or tried to shut out – now they were back, whether they admitted it or not. At first no one dared to look at them, scared as they were of hurting Martha, but then she herself began talking about the days when Sebastian came to the bakery for the first time – about his love for music and the stage and how shy he had been.

Once the taboo had been lifted, the stories cascaded over each other and the sisters embraced those long-gone days, hugging them tight like a favourite doll or teddy bear. Each sister had her own perspective on Sebastian, and each one dredged up different memories.

One evening Martha strode into the kitchen, making a gesture with her hands as if trying to stretch out a half-dried piece of chewing gum. She raised one arm to the yellowed ceiling and said, 'N-O-T-H-I-N-G,' making the word three times as long as its seven letters would normally require. 'Nothing . . . weighs so heavy as a fleck of dust that eludes you,' she declaimed in a pompous voice.

I wondered what had got into her – Martha never did anything mad or extravagant. Her sisters turned towards her with surprise as well, but burst into laughter when they realized what she was doing. They all began quoting disconnected sentences that didn't seem to refer to anything but which they all understood effortlessly because of the elaborate memories that went with them. They were lines from the plays Sebastian had rehearsed endlessly in this very kitchen. He had said the sentences in hundreds of different ways, changing them slightly until he had hit on just the right tone. When the week of the performance came – mostly sometime in the autumn, a few weeks after the fair – he would have the local audiences under his spell for three whole days. He played young lovers driven mad by desire and old fathers bent down under guilt and remorse. He could be a drunkard who got the whole audience laughing or a pitiful character who had everyone reaching for their handkerchiefs.

I didn't know any of this, but the sight of my aunts traipsing theatrically around the kitchen inspired me to do my bit as well. I stood in the middle of the room, looked from one to the other, then announced in a voice I had wrapped in a velvet cloth:

> Old Mother Misery as poor as a mouse,
> Lived in a hovel instead of a house,
> Yet behind that hovel there grew through her cares,
> A tree that was burdened with thousands of pears.

It was a verse by a Belgian poet I had learned at school, and it was so popular with the nuns that they asked me to recite it on all kinds of occasions. No one knew it at home. School and home had always been separate worlds for me. But now – I felt a compulsion welling up from my belly – I wanted my aunts to hear it and declaimed all the verses about the old woman who trapped Death in her pear tree so that no one could die, 'if even a wagon drove, crunch, over his throat'.

I didn't achieve the desired effect. The women stared at me in an astonished silence. Martha had gone as white as a sheet.

'More and more like Sebastian,' she whispered and left the kitchen.

I didn't understand what I had done wrong and looked from one to the other anxiously.

'Where did you learn to do that?' asked Christina.

'Ah, nowhere,' I blurted and went up to the attic to see if I could find any books that would be worth reading again because I had forgotten what happened in them.

Without telling Martha, I began asking people about my father. Often the events they came up with had nothing to do with Sebastian. The men remembered the beauty or voluptuousness of the girls who had now become anxious mothers. Men whose marriages had ebbed into indifference told me how often they went to bars seeking solace for their lost boyhood dreams. They tried to outdo each other with stories about how drunk they got during carnival or the village fairs and how they had thrown up all over staircases and bedroom rugs and left them stinking of stale beer for months. And they roared with laughter when they went on to say that their wives hadn't spoken to them for weeks afterwards.

Time had tinged the stories. Some people described my father as a timid organist who gave piano lessons to girls who were doomed to become wrinkled old spinsters before their time. Others presented him as a passionate man who must have seduced scores of women because – and here they gave me a conspiratorial wink – 'didn't he run off leaving a bun in the baker's daughter's oven?' It seemed as if no one in the whole village remembered whose child I was.

After Mass I went to the café to question the sacristan and the brewer, who was still a Sunday-afternoon regular. I visited the older band members and the amateur actors of the theatrical society, but gradually lost my way in a labyrinth of disconnected stories. My picture of Sebastian was like a tattered book that had fallen apart and been put back together in the wrong order.

When Martha was still with us a month after Oma's funeral, I asked her when she was going back home.

'I am home,' she said.

'Isn't your home with your husband?' I asked.

She shrugged.

'Don't you love him any more?'

'That's not the kind of question a girl should ask her mother,' she answered coolly.

'I want to know. Do you love him more than you loved my father? Did you actually love my father? Was I an accident? Were you drunk, or what? Did he rape you?'

'God no,' she said, giggling.

'Is it because it's all coming back to you? Is that why you're staying?'

'Don't ask so many questions. I love my husband, but him and Sebastian ... they're all mixed up, now that he's come back ... I need to think ... I feel guilty about Sebastian ...'

'Why did you let him go? What did you do to him? Why didn't he want to stay with you?'

'Please, stop it. I don't know any more. Some things just happen. You can't control them.'

'Like getting pregnant with me?'

'My God, I was so ashamed!'

'Did you ever stop being ashamed of me?'

'I was ashamed of Sebastian as well. He didn't do the

things a man should do. He had beautiful clothes, but he never saved up for furniture. He always wanted to touch me in front of other people, that was embarrassing. When we were alone, in his room or in the laundry, I liked it, but after we got married it was different. He forgot that there was work to do.'

'He did his work, didn't he?'

'Sure, hours playing the organ practising pieces he already knew back to front. He went to the band rehearsals and he rehearsed plays. That's not work. We had to order coal for the oven and I wanted a pram to take you out for walks. He didn't do things like that.'

'And your new husband? Does he do things like that?'

'He does everything. I don't need to do a thing any more. I've got a cleaning woman and someone else for the laundry. All I'm allowed to do is cook. I've got the whole day to knit and read. Do you know what that feels like when you've always had to work all day? It sounds lovely, because there was never any time for those things here, but if I spend the whole day knitting, I can't stop thinking about you here. Here, there's always something that needs doing, and there I was, wasting my time with things that weren't necessary. I felt guilty because someone else was cleaning the toilet while I was sitting on the sofa. I knitted jumpers for the missions so that I'd at least be doing something useful, but when I took them in to the nuns, they said that Africa was too hot for jumpers. I've got jumpers for an orphanage and no one wants to wear them.'

'Why didn't you ever knit a jumper for me? I could have used some warmth.'

'What do you mean? Why are you saying it like that?'

'Mama, I missed you. I didn't have a father and you weren't a mother to me either.'

She looked at me angrily. 'You mustn't say that. We always looked after you.'

'You didn't look after me. You never read stories to me, you never went to parent-teacher evenings. Christina read to me and Oma went walking with me on the heath. Vincentia taught me how to swim. Why didn't we ever go on holiday together?'

'We didn't have the time or the money. If things had been different, we would have had more choice. When I finally had more time, you didn't want to be with me. It's not fair to blame me.'

'What would you have done if I had come to live with you, Mama?'

'I'm not sure. Don't ask such weird questions. You never let on that you were unhappy. You didn't need me. You were always off playing by yourself with your books or singing songs you'd made up that I wasn't allowed to hear; you always stopped the moment you saw me.'

'And I wasn't allowed to be like Sebastian?'

She stared at me for a long time. 'Do you know how many people get to be organists and how many earn their living on building sites? I wanted to protect you.'

She walked away. She didn't want me to see that she was crying. I wasn't supposed to know that mothers cry too.

Twenty

I asked Christina whether the sisters had all been in love with Sebastian. We were doing the dishes and alone in the kitchen. Christina was washing up and I was drying the plates and cups she put down on the draining board. It was not the kind of question I was used to asking, but I had so many, and since Sebastian's death I had been unable to keep the lid on the box I had always packed them away in.

After I had whispered the question into my tea towel, Christina stood there for a moment with her hands in the dishwater. 'No,' she said after a while. 'I don't think so. I admired him. With me, it was more jealousy. I wanted to act as well, but wasn't able to, the theatrical society was for the elite . . . you know . . . for the brewer's sisters and the girls from the brickyard.'

'Weren't you allowed to join? Was it against the rules?'

'Not officially. It just wasn't the done thing. We didn't go on to secondary school in town either. I would have loved to continue my education . . .'

'And if you had? Would you have got a job away from the bakery?'

'We had to work here,' she said, staring straight ahead. 'I

don't think I could have left Martha alone. I never would have done that.'

'But why did you want to go to secondary school then? What did you want to learn?'

'Languages. I wanted to learn foreign languages and talk to people from other countries. And I wanted to travel. Maybe I could have become a writer. Of children's books. I had so many stories.'

She splashed the plates around in the dishwater and forgot that she was supposed to be washing them. 'If it hadn't been for the bakery, I might have got a job in a kindergarten. It's so lovely being around children. Children believe in the impossible, they never think about tomorrow, it's too far away. Tomorrow is a fairy tale, anything could happen tomorrow. Children don't bother with their surroundings. Have you ever seen a little boy playing with a train? He doesn't look at the end of the track. He just starts somewhere and can get stuck there for hours. He doesn't care that the train actually has to get to the station. Do you understand?'

I nodded, but didn't have a clue what she was talking about.

Christina said, 'Martha and I always had to worry about tomorrow. But you know, no matter how much you look into the future, tomorrow never comes any closer. I thought it would all happen once I was together with Jannes. He was happy for me to go to evening school. Who knows, I might have ended up writing books.'

I looked at Christina again, standing there with her hands in the dishwater and thinking about how things might have been, and it was as if my eyes were playing tricks on me. Christina split into two, and beside the woman in a blue-checked apron, there appeared a second Christina, dressed in an elegant suit, with golden earrings and a horn hairslide in her dark brown hair. She smiled at me and showed me a book with a picture of a child in a handcart on the cover. She put the book down on the table and walked into the hall. The door swung on its hinges behind her.

Christina's life had been shaped by unwritten rules. It was not forbidden for a baker's daughter to go to school in the city, it was just unusual. None of the nonsense you learned there would help you when it came to selling bread or stoning cherries for the fair-time tarts. The family's fourth daughter had spent her whole life staring down the tunnel but had never found the courage to go through it. Time and again, Christina had laid her dreams between the blue wrapping of the wedding suit she had never worn, and when she finally tried to realize them they had turned to dust. I knew she could have been a writer, even without going to secondary school, because nowhere could you learn to tell stories better than by listening to her. For weddings and birthdays she often composed poems that were so long she needed to write them on a roll of wallpaper. But when she read them, no one was bored for even a second. She was also responsible for the advertisements we placed in the local newspaper in the run-up to the fairs or Christmas. She wrote them in verse and sometimes they were so witty that we quoted parts of them on signs in the shop. Once a rhyming advertisement she had written for the Feast of Saint Nicholas won a prize from the Small Businessmen's Association.

When I told her that she could still write, that all she needed to do was buy a second-hand typewriter the next time the town hall was selling off their used office supplies, she replied that it was too late, it was even too late for her to learn to type.

I clipped out a newspaper advertisement that promised to teach you how to write in a single weekend in a cloister in the south of the country, under the guidance of a well-known female author of romantic novels. We joined forces and finally talked her into going there. What we didn't know was that the weekend was for bored rich widows and unhappily married women in search of new diversions. It was not surprising that Christina felt unhappy among them and that her embarrassed imagination crept into the dark oak wardrobe and pulled the door shut behind it. She didn't get a word down on the page and saw her failure as confirmation that opportunity had passed her by.

Christina insisted that I avoid the same pitfalls. She demanded that I be sent to secondary school in town, something Martha thought ridiculous. Their disagreement led to bickering.

'Why should she learn things she won't need in the shop?' asked Martha, when Christina was back on her hobbyhorse.

'You have to give her a chance to improve herself. Then

she can decide for herself whether or not she works in the shop,' answered Christina.

'What else can she do?'

'*What else can she do*? As if your life is all mapped out just because you happen to be born in a bakery!'

'I think it is. Lots of things are determined in advance,' said Martha pensively.

'There are ways of breaking the pattern,' Christina insisted.

'But that takes courage, and you have no way of knowing that it will be worth the effort,' Martha answered. 'Who's to say you've made the right decision?'

'If you leave it to someone else to decide, it can't possibly be right.'

'But it's easy to leave it to someone else, because then you can always blame them if things don't turn out the way you wanted,' Martha replied. 'Is Emma supposed to make up for something you didn't do?'

Christina was silent.

I didn't like them fighting about me. I didn't really care whether I went to secondary school or the domestic science school. I was actually glad not to have to go to town, because that would have meant getting up an hour earlier to cycle to school with the others. In the summer it would have been fun – you'd see the dawn and watch wisps of mist doing their last ghostly dance before hiding in the treetops until night returned – but in the months when the days were short, when the wind came from the north and cut your cheeks like a knife, no coat or hat could keep you warm.

Martha wanted me to go to the Small Businessmen's Family Association, an organization that arranged fortnightly cultural get-togethers for the children of the local shopkeeping elite. Sometimes there would be readings on the customs of exotic tribes or about religions other than Catholicism. They ran excursions to exhibitions in Liège in Belgium or Aachen in Germany. Martha sent me along to meet people my own age and Christina hoped that it would fill the gaps in my education, but it was all way over my head. I was unsure about the direction my life was taking – my choices seemed limited.

I had inherited none of the dedication of my aunts. My knitting was worse than Oma's and even sloppier. I couldn't sew like Camilla. Clara's tireless explanations of the grafting and propagation of plants had all been in vain. I had been scared of the horses when we delivered the bread with a wagon, and now I had a phobia of cars, something I might have developed because of Anne's driving style in the days when there were only a few of us living at the bakery and we went out on Sunday drives – she was so captivated by the landscape that she couldn't keep her eyes on the road and was constantly having to swerve to avoid trees and ditches. I couldn't embroider like Aunt Marie – although embroidered sheets had become so unfashionable that that wasn't really such a disaster.

*

Marie herself had also given up her obsession for cross-stitching. In the convent she had let her embroidery needles rust and discovered a new passion – cooking. The dishes she had learned to prepare filled us with astonishment as they wandered over our tongues. Every meal she made was a new experience. We now heard for the first time that the bishop had made a habit of entertaining guests in Marie's convent. The princes of the Church were connoisseurs of food and drink, and in the convent's kitchens she had learned to prepare the most exquisite dishes – sauces with unpronounceable names and meat dishes that were so extra-ordinary we spent the whole evening struggling to find words that would do them justice. We had never known that you could do anything more to potatoes than boil or fry them, but Marie turned a humble spud into an exotic vegetable whose taste surpassed our wildest dreams. She had also become an expert on French and Italian wines, but this knowledge proved less useful – in our village people only drank beer and gin.

Marie tried to draw me into her culinary activities. Her efforts failed, but she took advantage of our time together to talk with me. She told me her own story, the story of the things that had happened to her and had forced her to continually postpone her marriage and ultimately end it after such a brief period.

Marie was just seventeen when she met the man she wanted as a husband and as a father for her children. It was at the village fair and he was tall and strong. He worked at the brickyard and his hands were rough, but since they were the only male hands Marie had ever known, she simply assumed that all men's hands were like that. She accepted the fact that she walked around with a chafed chin for days after they had kissed and she prayed every day to God that he would provide her with a family with aunts and uncles who dropped in for a cup of tea on Sundays. She also prayed to God that her husband would stay with her all the days of her life, until their children had children of their own and were able to care for them themselves, and preferably no more than three.

Every evening Marie went up to her bedroom early to say her prayers. Until the day a girlfriend gave her an educational booklet about modern family life. Her faith was shaken to its foundations by the illustrations of copulating couples and women in labour and the discovery that the first intercourse of man and woman was a painful and bloody event. Marie was so upset that she seized the rough wooden crucifix she had bought during mission week to help the poor Negroes who had made it, and begged God to spare her. She waved the primitive cross around wildly and gave herself over to her prayers with such a passion that she lost her balance and fell upon the cross, injuring her vagina so seriously that she began to bleed terribly. She stanched the bleeding with a towel and bandaged her loins so tightly with a cloth that it took days before she could walk again. The injured tissue grew together so skewed and crooked that a male member would never be able to find its way in. The doctor who later examined her because of recurring infections told her that she needed an operation, but Marie was too scared to arrange one.

And so she married, under pressure from an unknowing Martha, with a horrible secret between her legs that obliged her to keep her husband at a distance – until the day he tried to take her by force. She fled the house, spent the whole night shivering on the edge of the marsh, and the next day she picked up her things and returned to the bakery.

'There was so much blood,' she said, 'it was running over the floor and it was all over my clothes. I spent days washing my hands but it still stuck to them. It got everywhere, onto my needles, into my silk, I embroidered it into all those sheets and pillowcases.' She had to laugh, because bent over a convent stove she had finally shaken the smell of that blood. It was the first time I had seen her laugh. Marie's mouth was not made for laughter.

Her story had nothing to do with my father, but it still gave me a better insight into the things I had witnessed as a child but never understood.

Marie had come back from the convent a more talkative woman. One day when I caught her alone in the kitchen with a bottle of gin, she told me the whole story over again.

I asked her why she had entered the convent.

Thoughtfully she explained, 'I don't know any more. After Martha left, the heart of the house stopped beating. I felt so alone. I thought I would be able to have better conversations with God in the convent. Here someone was always butting in with idle chatter . . . But I don't believe He listened to me any better there.'

'You learned to do something you enjoy doing. That wouldn't have happened here,' I said.

She looked at me for a moment before replying, 'You're right, you know. I should actually do more with it. Maybe I could cook for weddings. Then I would have a profession after all. Goodness, do you think He did hear my prayers?'

According to local custom, weddings, Holy Communions and funerals were celebrated at home and someone was hired to prepare the meals so that the entire family could relax and enjoy the party.

Marie's idea would come to fruition sooner than she could have guessed.

I asked her if she wanted to have the operation now, after all, but she started giggling and said that she already had. She told me that she had shared her cell with an older nun who had made a habit of creeping into her bed because the nights were so cold. When the gentle fingers that whispered over her skin were unable to find the softness of her vagina, the other nun brought the matter up with the Mother Superior, who sent Marie to hospital to have the fused tissues repaired.

The doctors had been unable to restore her fully, but afterwards she would have been able to go to bed with a man – if she had wanted to. But even wanting to was something she could no longer imagine. She had erased all memories of her husband from her mind, and fear had prevented her from drawing any new pictures.

The new love of her life was many times more erotic than its predecessor. She poured her newly discovered sensuality into her sauces and soups and it was a struggle for the wedding and funeral guests not to abandon all etiquette and start licking their plates. They tasted a passion that had simmered for more than twenty years and was juicier than the most delicious casserole.

Unexpectedly, Marie was asked to cook dinner for the wedding of the new mayor after the woman who had always done the catering on such occasions broke her leg. This one job led to more and more requests for formal meals or buffet dinners. Since there was too much work for her alone, she started taking Anne along to help.

Without any special effort or planning on their parts, their collaboration grew into a prospering business. Two lonely sisters befriended each other at an age when they had already reconciled themselves to solitude. And by opening up to each other, they also became better companions for the other sisters. The family grew closer than ever before and the sisters became even more important to each other.

Despite spending more time preparing food, Anne began to diet. The formless lump she had been for years melted away to reveal a body with the soft curves of a woman in the prime of life. She still suffered from an allergy to lacy underwear and had no choice but to continue buying simple cotton knickers and bras, but for the rest of her wardrobe, she now went to a Maastricht boutique that specialized in French fashion.

After she had regained the figure she had had when working at the mayor's and was able to dress normally again, other feelings and desires began to creep over Anne's skin. She started advertising in lonely hearts columns.

It became a new addiction. She began with occasional

advertisements in the regional daily but soon progressed to national newspapers, which provided a much better harvest of letters. Giggling, she discussed the authors' merits with Marie and Christina. There were always a few interesting reactions in each pile, and with these she would begin a correspondence, often with the assistance of Christina, who provided her with sentences she would never have come up with alone. She used this safe method of attraction and seduction until the men insisted on a meeting, whereupon she dedicated a number of letters to the details of where and when, and how she envisaged their encounter.

Only once did she actually meet one of these correspondents. She had always stopped before things got that far, because the closer the encounter came the more it made her think of the mayor. Then she would write, with Christina's help, that she had decided not to go through with it after all.

The one time she did make a date, she went with Marie. After just ten minutes, they told the man that they had to leave to go to hospital to wait by their father's deathbed.

Twenty-one

In the autumn, a few months after we had buried Oma, I saw her again at the top of the cellar stairs.

'Oma! What are you doing here?' I asked.

'It is sauerkraut time already,' said Oma. Her accent had not changed a bit, but she was wearing a navy-blue dress I had never seen before. Her grey hair was plaited and pinned up, making her look years younger.

She walked down into the cellar. I followed, but she had disappeared between the shelves of fruit and vegetable preserves.

Every autumn Oma had filled grey stoneware pots with finely grated cabbage and salt. She had then placed a board on top of the cabbage, and a stone on top of the board to weigh it down and press the liquid out of the cabbage. But there was more to it. She had also added herbs and spices, and no one else knew which ones or, more importantly, in which proportions. Every year we had told each other that we needed to write the recipe down for posterity. But everyone had always acted as if Oma would live for ever and no one had ever grabbed a notebook or taken the trouble of committing the ingredients to memory.

*

A week later she sat down next to me in the kitchen while I was peeling potatoes.

'You are peeling too deep, always the same with you,' she grumbled.

'If you can do better, go ahead,' I snapped. I had been left to peel the potatoes by myself, because everyone had gone to the town hall to attend a meeting explaining the new traffic circulation plan and why they were thinking of closing our street.

Oma laughed. 'I don't need to do that no more. Saturday we are making sauerkraut,' she said in a determined voice.

'Oma, nobody knows how. We forgot to write it down,' I said.

'You think maybe I forget? I will tell you,' she said. 'Saturday.' And with that, she walked into the hall.

I asked Martha if we should make some sauerkraut, but she thought it was too much trouble and said that from now on we would buy it at the greengrocer's. She seemed to have forgotten that the greengrocer had always bought pots from us so that his customers would have an alternative to the usual mass-produced product. There was no doubt about which of the two was better: although there had never been any official tests, Oma's sauerkraut had much the better reputation. Nonetheless, Christina agreed with Martha and didn't feel like cluttering the cellar with pots of sauerkraut, even though we were used to it, and the bricks of the cellar walls were so drenched with the smell of fermentation that it still rose up years later when the house was knocked down by the developer's bulldozers. When

Saturday came, I didn't have any white cabbage to fill the pots. I knew that Oma would be angry and I avoided the kitchen because that was where I expected to see her.

Suddenly she appeared behind me while I was hanging freshly ironed clothes in the wardrobe.

'Don't think you can walk away from me,' she said sternly and followed me around until I couldn't stand it any more and started talking to Marie about the sauerkraut, but without mentioning Oma. I asked her whether she didn't need some sometimes for her dinners and suggested that it would reflect better on her if she had some of her own, made at home to an old family recipe. I lied that I knew how Oma had made it.

Marie was grateful for the idea and ordered a mountain of white cabbage, which she, Anne and I grated in two days with the big wooden cucumber grater. We ended up with two laundry baskets full and were able to fill all ten of the stoneware pots Oma had always used.

Oma told me exactly how many cloves and elderberries to add without either of my aunts noticing her presence. Marie wanted to add more cloves and Anne wanted to add bay leaves, but Oma began waving her arms furiously and I called out that that wasn't right. Anne said that she was sure it was okay. Oma shoved me in the back to let me know I had to stop her. This difficult Saturday afternoon concluded with a compromise between the new cuisine and the dead past.

I saw Oma more and more often. At first I thought that it had something to do with my periods. The last few days before it came, I was always light-headed and felt as though I were floating on air. I thought that might have explained my seeing things that weren't normal. But there were times when Oma came every day, and at other times she could stay away for ages. Mostly she walked silently through the house and only smiled or shook her head when she saw that I was making a mess of something.

'Sebastian is worrying himself that you are not going to the good school. You should be making more music.'

'Tell him to tell Martha that,' I answered.

'You cannot give Martha the blame for everything,' she said and disappeared through the outside wall.

Oma started to enjoy passing through closed windows and thick walls. At first she had opened the doors and used them the way she had while still alive. Now she took to appearing suddenly before me and sniggering, 'To go through walls is really fun.'

'It's no fun for me when you keep making me jump like that,' I answered angrily.

Twenty-two

Martha phoned her husband every Saturday evening to tell him about events in the bakery, where she was gradually taking over all her former tasks. Her husband didn't come for Sunday dinner the way he had in the days before their wedding, and Martha didn't invite him to either.

Almost seven weeks after Oma's death, she received an emergency call summoning her to the hospital in Maastricht – her husband had suffered a heart attack. He was in more of a hurry than his wife. By the time Martha arrived at the hospital with Vincentia at the wheel of the delivery van, the nurses were getting ready to take him down to the morgue. A week later Martha came home with a stack of papers the notary had given her. Since her husband had never made a will, she had now, as his lawfully wedded wife, inherited everything: the house, the company, the company vehicles and his private car, a black Mercedes.

'What am I supposed to do with it all?' she asked. 'I'm not going to live in that big house by myself, and I don't know a thing about dried fruit.' She put the documents away in a cupboard and ignored them.

She didn't speak about her husband any more either. When we were playing rummy on Sunday evening and asked her what she had done with her husband on Sundays, she replied, 'Nothing,' and simply laid out her cards – she won surprisingly often.

I knew that she had a television and suggested moving it to our house, but she mumbled that it was all just sports programmes, whereas I knew that they also broadcast films and plays – a girl at school had told me.

A month after Martha had put the documents in the cupboard, Christina got them out again and dumped them on the table in front of Martha.

'You can't just act as if they don't exist,' she said. 'The manager has been here. The salesmen want to be paid and they've run out of stock. The suppliers won't deliver until their bills are paid.'

'There isn't any manager,' answered Martha.

'Well Dré says he's the manager and he wants to buy the business now while it's still going well.'

'Let the notary arrange it all,' answered Martha.

'You have to negotiate a price first,' said Marie. 'It must be worth a lot.'

'What would I do with lots of money? It doesn't even feel like it's rightfully mine. I didn't earn it.'

'Give it to me then,' mumbled Marie, whose time in the convent had done nothing to reduce her love of money.

For three weeks Martha acted as if she had forgotten about the business – until Dré appeared at the door, a big man with square shoulders and an unfamiliar accent. After a long conversation in the living room, Martha packed a bag and went off with him. Two weeks passed before she came back in the van with Vincentia.

Day after day, Martha had wandered the long halls and empty rooms of that big house listening to the sound of her sisters' laughter. A thousand times she asked herself whether it was better to sell dried fruit or fresh bread. She walked past objects that had never been hers, and now that they were hers, she didn't know whether she should love them, and she wondered whether her sisters might grow to love them – there were so many things that were foreign to the bakery.

Every day she moved something into the hall. Last of all, she moved the television there too. Then she went to the notary and handed over the documents for the house and the business.

The strong smell of fresh bread had won out over the scentless dried fruit. The man who had promoted himself to manager took over both house and business, plus the company van and the black Mercedes (this was something Marie never stopped complaining about – during her days as a nun she had developed a predilection for big black cars).

An antique dealer came to clear out the rooms and gave Martha so much money that it wouldn't even fit in her purse. On a Wednesday afternoon, she called for Vincentia to come and pick her up. They packed the contents of the hall into the back of the van and then unloaded it all into the kitchen at home.

*

Martha knew her sisters' desires well and had carefully chosen the things she brought back from the city. I was given a fat, leather-bound encyclopaedia. She brought two laundry baskets full of wool, although hand-knitted pullovers were going out of fashion. In the corner of the kitchen were five boxes of books, mainly German novels, and we chuckled that it was going to be a long, romantic winter.

While we were all still happily looking at our presents and feeling a warm glow in our hearts, Martha set a big case full of bottles down on the table. The sisters sipped the liqueurs and spirits from tiny crystal glasses that Martha had brought back with her as well. We tasted every bottle – I was allowed to lick my aunts' empty glasses – and were astounded to discover that alcohol could come in so many flavours. Only Marie knew better – she always told us which bottle to try next.

We got all giggly and gasped for breath as the drink burnt the backs of our throats.

With everyone's eyes still watering, Martha laid her bulging purse on the table and raised a glass of green Benedictine for a toast.

'I'm rich,' she giggled, slurring her words. 'I'm a rich widow.' She laughed so much she could hardly speak and her sisters raised their glasses. 'But I've got a plan,' she went on at last. 'I want a beautiful shop. We're going to have the most beautiful bakery in the whole province!'

And everyone drank to that as well.

Martha explained at length the plans she had crafted during the empty nights in the big house. The sisters listened patiently. They knew that their sister always needed an awful lot of words to explain something. For hours Martha spoke about the changing economy and a new generation of customers with new expectations and wishes.

When the moon had had enough of waiting for the end of her speech and had withdrawn behind the clouds, which would keep the sun covered this day as well, Martha finally got down to the nitty-gritty. She wanted a supermarket. A shop like the one the big grocery chain had built next to the church. A place where customers served themselves and paid at a checkout.

That day there was no fresh bread.

Perfectly straight-faced, Christina explained to the customers that a man from the city had shown up at the crack of dawn and had bought all the bread to take to a village in the Eifel where the villagers had never eaten fresh bread because there was no baker in the village and they were forced to make a trip down the valley once a week by donkey cart to buy a week's supply at a time, which they then warmed up in their tiled ovens . . . Christina was so convincing that everyone believed her.

And that was how the village got a new myth: the story of the Mysterious Bread Buyer.

The contractor made several alternative plans before the sisters settled on rebuilding almost the entire ground floor as a shop. With the exception of a small section that would serve as a storeroom, the garage was to be incorporated in the shop as well. The staircase to the bedrooms was to be moved to the back of the house. Downstairs, only the kitchen remained private. One of the front bedrooms on the first floor became the new living room, and since we had plenty of money, a new lounge suite was bought with two extra armchairs so that everyone could relax in front of the new TV. We even got wall-to-wall carpets so we could walk around barefoot without freezing our toes.

The bakery got a new oven so that Marie could bake the fancy French pastries she had learned about during a course in town.

The festive opening of the new shop was held two months later. The floor was full of hydrangeas sent by other shop-keepers. As was the custom, the priest arrived to bless the premises, although Martha still gagged at the sight of a member of the cloth. The new mayor dropped by to wish the women success, and I gave every child that came into the shop a gas-filled balloon with the name of the shop printed on it and a postcard on a string that they could write their name on before releasing the balloon outside. The postcard that was posted back from furthest away was to win a three-storey cake for the child's next birthday – something that never happened because someone was cunning enough to send the card to relatives in New Zealand with the request that they post it back from there. Just when Marie was about to start work on the cake, someone told her that balloons couldn't possibly float that far, but by that time all the other cards had been thrown away and it was impossible to find out which balloon really had got the furthest.

*

The first Christmas in our new living room was unforgettable. Under the Christmas tree that the nurseryman had delivered, Christina made a papier-mâché grotto for the Holy Family. Next to this, on a coffee table, she laid out a field of dried moss for the shepherds and their sheep. She hid tiny mirrors under the moss as ponds. Christina gave me money to buy ten woolly sheep to put down beside the porcelain lambs.

When all the balls, bells and birds were hanging in the tree, Martha made a ceremonial entry with a long box in her arms. She set it down on the table and looked at us all. 'Unwrap it,' she said, and from between the tissue paper I pulled out a Christmas-tree decoration of unimaginable beauty. I had never seen it before. Sebastian had bought it just before leaving. It had never been used.

Marie and Anne made a dinner that took us half a day to eat. Camilla had decorated the table with satin ribbons and bows of red and white tulle. Clara had brought pine branches from the nursery and she and Vincentia had hung them up all over the house. Christina and I had written a Christmas story. We started reading it during the meal and were still reading it long after we had finished eating.

Everyone was now used to my way of reciting, and when the candles in the tree had been replaced for the second time, Camilla brought her mandolin down from the attic. After she had tuned it, we sang Christmas carols until early in the morning, with Oma humming along at the back of the room.

Twenty-three

At first I was the only one who saw Oma, but one after-noon, when we were in the middle of a heated discussion on the stairs, Christina suddenly appeared below us in the hall, rigid with fright and staring at the scene. From then on the others began seeing her as well, and in time she became an ordinary aspect of day-to-day life that everyone took for granted.

Often she sat quietly in the corner of the kitchen watching us. At other times we saw her shuffling through the bed-rooms or sitting on the stairs for hours at a time. The only place that was off limits was the shop: if she appeared there we shooed her away – she had never hung around there when she was alive either.

I desperately wanted to know why she kept on coming back, but despite the urgency of my questions, she hardly ever answered. I asked her if she was a lost soul. If she had committed some mortal sin that barred her from admission to heaven.

'You do not even know what heaven is, you go too much to church,' was all she said.

'But what are you doing here?'

'You ask too much questions.'

'Is Sebastian with you?' I said insistently. 'Can you tell me what he was like?'

'Listen to your inside, you know already what he was like.'

'But everyone tells me different things, Oma,' I said frantically.

'Yes, people are not always the same. They look at others through their own eyes,' she said, confusing me totally.

Sometimes she didn't say a word and sometimes she was with people we didn't know. We didn't let that bother us either. But when my grandfather suddenly appeared beside her, my aunts dropped what they were doing and got so upset that they weren't able to do a stitch of work for the rest of the day. They were overcome by an ominous foreboding.

'Beware the fat lady,' Oma said, walking into the bakery with the sisters' father.

Three weeks later, an overweight Flemish woman appeared in the shop with a mongoloid son and a man in a grey suit. The woman's skin was the colour of old newspaper and she had run a blue rinse through her hair.

She introduced herself to Christina as the baker's widow and said that the house and business were hers – 'according to law'.

The man in grey nodded: he was a lawyer and had come to explain to the sisters that the bakery and half of the shop belonged to the widow and that her son also had a right to a share of the other half: together they owned more than fifty per cent and it was only logical that she should move into the house and be supported by the proceeds of the business . . .

The woman with blue hair and a yellowed face had been married to the father of the seven sisters for more than two decades. He had often told her about his big house, his bakery and his shop, and many times he had promised to move there with her. It was just one of those things they had never got around to, but now that he was no longer with them, she had decided to come and look after his 'lassies', as she put it. She gestured at the two worn suitcases she had brought with her and at her retarded son, who was now finally able to meet his half-sisters.

Each of the seven sisters had secretly hoped for the return of the father most of them had hardly known, but none of their fantasies had included a new wife. Silently they led the Flemish woman and her retinue into the kitchen. She offered the family a spongy hand to shake, then sat down on Grandpa's chair and pulled her son onto her lap, something he was far too old for.

'Take the suitcases to my room,' the woman commanded when Vincentia offered her a cup of coffee.

The sisters looked at each other. The bedrooms had been reallocated after the renovations and each of them now had a bed of their own. One of the sisters settled down each night in the woolly valley of a mattress that was left over from the days when they had curled up against each other; another slept in a new narrow bed that Vincentia and the cabinetmaker had made to the measurements of a modern spring mattress – you couldn't snuggle down into it but it was better for your back. Everyone had made their choice between old-fashioned warmth and modern comfort. Martha was the only one who slept in a room by herself, in the cubbyhole next to the stairs. Anne and Marie shared the room that had once been their parents' bedroom, and Christina, Vincentia and I slept in the remaining room at the front of the house. The twins slept in the attic, in narrow beds that left enough room for Camilla's sewing machine.

Three cups of coffee and six muffins later, when no one had shown any sign of wanting to show her her room, the widow stamped upstairs by herself to inspect the rest of the house. She walked from room to room, stared for a long time out of the window, then finally announced that the front room was for her, for her alone. With a double bed, because she wasn't used to sleeping in a single. Her son was to have Martha's room, she gurgled; after all, he was the son and heir, the only male descendant. She waited. The sisters looked at the young man who was supposedly their half-brother and were overcome by a sense of shame, as if they were somehow responsible for the defective chromosomes of this overgrown child who smiled at them and let the dribble run down over the collar of his pullover.

Martha shuddered. Her father might have got drunk now and then, but in his whole life he had never worn a jacket with as much as the slightest fleck of grease on it – she couldn't imagine him living under the same roof with these people. Of all the things she remembered about her father, the most striking was suddenly an image of a man with a long, waxed moustache, a shirt with a high, starched collar and a tie with a broad knot. On Sundays he had always worn a waistcoat and he had never left the house without his bowler and his cane. The cane went with his jaunty step; he never took it as a precaution for later, when he would come wobbling homeward after celebrating his self-imposed Sunday obligations at the bar of the Harmonie.

No matter how inappropriate this woman was for the father Martha had known, the documents she presented told another story. Martha set her sense of repugnance aside and thought of all the times she had knelt in the chapel of Our Lady of Perpetual Help and prayed to Mary for a new mother. That mother was now standing in their kitchen. Martha looked upon it as a late mercy and realized that it would be a sin to question it.

Beds and bedding were dragged about the house all afternoon and by dinnertime a place had been made for their stepmother. She was given Christina's bed. Martha's bed came into our room. Anne's double bed went up to the attic, where Vincentia would share it with Clara, and Anne herself was to share a bed with Marie. The retarded halfbrother was given the first bed Vincentia had made with the cabinetmaker. Vincentia had resisted this plan fiercely, but Martha said it was ridiculous to be so attached to a bed.

It was strange to be suddenly living together with people we didn't know, even if they were family. There was nothing motherly about the fat woman. She was constantly calling out in her blue-rinsed voice that it was her right and her house. No one disputed this, although none of them had realized that their father had remained the legal owner all these years, even despite the major renovation paid for with Martha's inheritance. Similarly, it had not occurred to any of them that their father might have remarried and that such a marriage would confer rights that seemed unfair emotionally.

None of the sisters had ever drawn anything more than pocket money from their share of the business. Martha had always taken care of the finances, both for the bakery and the household. They had all handed their wages over to Martha, who had used the money to pay the suppliers' bills and the various taxes. It was Martha who decided whose turn it was for a new overcoat or when it was time to buy a new bicycle. Everyone paid for smaller purchases out of their pocket money, and anything that was left was deposited in savings accounts. The Flemish woman was their stepmother and the freak was their half-brother, a child of their father, so they were both incorporated into the sisters' pattern of distribution according to need.

On Sunday, after the first bottle of gin, the woman was more at ease and began telling the sisters about their father and how he had gone to Belgium hoping that his wounds might heal. One day he would return, he said, going back to his girls and the bakery that was renowned far beyond the village boundaries. But a good opportunity never presented itself, and after he had married the maid of the baker he was working for, his hopes of returning faded. He had had another child with his new wife, and now, as his widow, she explained that for years she had been longing to introduce her son to his sisters. Now she finally had a chance to do so. She said that their father had not been exaggerating when he described how wonderful the business was, and she hoped that they would all become one big happy family.

Everyone nodded. Martha called the off-licence for another two bottles of gin, and after her fifth glass she began sobbing. I was given two glasses as well, diluted with water, and I'm not sure whether it was because of the alcohol or because she was actually there, but I saw Oma through the glass panes of the door. She was shaking her head.

The widow's sincere feelings were as phoney as the hair on the head of the senior master of the boys' school. All she wanted was to be waited on like a queen. It was not clear whether she was trying to perpetuate the way Grandpa had treated her, or whether she felt as if she was finally surrounded by enough vassals. Her son was the court jester and she demanded that he be treated with more respect than he deserved. Together the two of them soon began to get on the sisters' nerves.

After trying a new dish she had read about in a foreign magazine, Marie became the first to take the full brunt. The meal did not turn out perfectly, but there was nothing unusual about that – magazine editors often made mistakes in their recipes. Generally Marie would then discuss the recipe all evening with her sisters, listen to their suggestions and try an adjusted version the following day. It would already be much tastier, we would spend hours praising her, and with triumph glowing on her cheeks, she would go to bed to dream about the dish and search for the finesses that would ultimately yield a meal fit for a king.

This time Marie had made an Alsace meat speciality with Limburg asparagus. She had bought the first asparagus from a young bed, something which is always risky – you should actually wait a few weeks to see how the crop is responding to a new bed. The asparagus was not at its best, but in combination with the meat it was a 'true adventure'. That was Marie's explanation and we all laughed and joked about this new euphemism.

Only the widow remained silent. We had no way of knowing that she had never eaten asparagus before. She had nothing to compare it to and no way of judging its quality. The sisters' laughter worked on her sense of insecurity and made her feel like they were making fun of her. She hurled her plate through the room and screeched that it was 'the filthiest muck she had ever eaten'. The words she used were painfully at odds with Marie's fine cuisine.

Her son began to laugh and threw his plate at the wall as well. Then he picked up the serving dish with the rest of the asparagus and would have thrown that as well if Vincentia had not grabbed it in time.

Marie's face took on the colour of a starched apron. I thought she was going to pick up the bowl of mashed potatoes and throw it in the widow's face, and I think she would have as well, except that Martha took hold of her and said that we had to be understanding. After all, they *were* foreigners.

*

The seven sisters were not used to having a mother, and their ability to be understanding was subjected to daily buffeting. The widow settled into the kitchen just as Oma had done, but instead of Oma's chatter with its aroma of warm cocoa, her coarse Flemish voice blew frost over the tiles and chilled our hearts.

Her moronic son was always sticking his nose in where he had no business to be. He scooped handfuls of freshly whipped cream out of the bakery mixing bowls and scoffed it so greedily that he smeared it all over his ears, where it dried into a yellow crust. He ate the chocolates from the display case in the shop. He took bites out of tarts that were waiting to be delivered.

The widow said that anyone who laid a finger on him would answer to her – after all, he didn't understand that things like that weren't allowed. And she told the sisters that they should be grateful that she even let them stay in the house – they weren't her children after all. With that she spat on the floor, lit up a fat cigar, pulled a bottle of gin out of the cupboard and drank it down by herself in a couple of hours. Sometimes she shared the bottle with her mongoloid son, who became aggressive and started throwing chairs around.

The house began to defend itself against the intruders. The wallpaper started bubbling and black mould grew in the seams. It became harder and harder for Martha to see these monsters as the answer to her prayers. Their presence was an unfair punishment, but a voice that sounded like her father's told her that it was her duty to do what was asked of her.

One evening Marie finally opened her pinched mouth – that was the one thing about her that hadn't changed – to tell Martha that she didn't need to take care of *everything* their father had left behind. All Martha could do was shrug helplessly. She didn't know how to get rid of the widow.

In whispers, Martha began to protest the unthinkable cruelty God had inflicted upon her. But she didn't dare resist, if only because she didn't know how – it was something she had never learned.

In the end it was the widow herself who punched her so hard in the stomach that she gasped for breath and felt like hitting back. The fat Fleming said that it wasn't right for everyone to automatically eat from their combined income and suggested that the sisters begin paying board. She proposed a ridiculous amount of money. Furthermore, she demanded that she be given the money from the till and take over the responsibility of paying the bills. It was her business after all, as she said for the thousandth time.

The kitchen was so full of words that should never have been spoken that Martha had to go out into the hall to cough them up. Christina followed her out and put an arm around her shoulders.

'I always took care of things so well,' sobbed Martha, 'and now none of it's any good. I've given my whole life to the bakery and now it's not even mine.'

'It's all of ours,' said Vincentia, who had come out into the hall as well. 'We all worked here just as unhappily.'

'That's not true!' said Christina. 'We had great times and things have always been good. Don't suddenly start dragging it through the mud now. That would mean our whole lives have been pointless.'

'Right now it's no fun at all,' said Vincentia. 'I can't stand it any more. I'm leaving.'

'If anyone goes, we all go,' said Martha, suddenly drying her tears, because the widow had come out into the hall to see if anyone was going to answer her.

'Nobody around here pays board,' said Marie. 'We all work hard. You're the one who should be paying us. So in future shut your mouth and leave the money to Martha. And if you lay a finger on the money in the till, I'll chop it off.'

Everyone was astonished by the withering power in Marie's voice.

Unsure of herself, the widow looked from one to the other, but the sight of the broad grins on the sisters' faces intimidated her so much she was temporarily afraid to make any more demands.

Instead she increased her complaints about Marie's cooking. Once she even spat it out over the table to show how disgusting it was. She only did that once though, because Marie looked at her as if she would empty a boiling hot pan over her head if she committed such sacrilege again . . .

The cosy atmosphere drained out of the kitchen. After the dishes, everyone went their own way. Camilla went up to the attic to spend her evenings between white tulle and satin. She didn't spend all her time at the sewing machine –

more and more often she just stood at the mirror admiring herself in the wedding dress she was making. Clara came home very late because she worked at the nursery until dark and then ate with her boss. Vincentia spent more of her time in the cabinetmaker's workshop. When she couldn't do anything to help him, she would sit there drinking coffee and watching the master craftsman at work on the finest jobs the province had to offer.

Marie and Anne developed the habit of preparing their dinners in the bakery, after first locking it to make sure their half-brother couldn't get in to destroy the salads or contaminate the meat with his unwashed hands. Martha went to the living room to do the bookkeeping and adopted an icy silence when the widow came to join her at the table.

Sometimes Martha and Christina went walking with me to the marshes on the other side of the railway tracks. Here, between the copper-coloured streams, you could still hear the whispering of Roman legionaries who had been left behind in the days when Europe was awash with the mega-lomania of emperors. We passed time strolling between wrinkled tree trunks that were covered by rank creepers. Walking between the two sisters, I listened to them tell stories about their father that reflected the different images they had kept of him. Their tales of my grandfather were like two wanderers following the railway, with the two versions on opposite sides of the tracks.

Christina had woven an elegant story around the man in the photo she kept on her bedside table. The portrait showed a young man in a three-piece suit, seated in a photographer's studio, with a stylish moustache and a triumphant look in his eyes, a big cigar clamped between two fingers and his hands resting on a cane.

Martha's memories were burdened with anger, because she felt forced to do things that had always frightened her. In the years in which the pregnancies were destroying her mother's health, her father had become a stranger who raised his hand to her too often and with too little reason. When she was younger he had only lost control when he was nervous about things he preferred to ignore, but the man who finally left them was increasingly subject to unpredictable fits of rage. Despite his temper, Martha had always been convinced that her father was different from the men who came home drunk and beat their wives. But looking back, she began to doubt this picture. Her mother might never have had bruises, but Martha remembered the look in her eyes and how it finally came to resemble the expression she saw in the faces of the battered women who always came into the shop asking for another week's credit.

Listening to both sides, I was free to decide for myself what to commit to memory. Late at night or early in the morning, I updated my diary so that later I could tell my own children, if I ever had any, about the people who had shaped my childhood. I wanted to be sure that my children's lives would not become a stagnant river. I too was weaving my own story about the man who would be my children's grandfather, and I realized that I had different versions as well. I touched up the picture Martha had given me, because I knew that it wasn't the right colour, and gradually I transformed it into a man I could recognize, if only because he was my opposite: if a hall full of people had looked at me,

I would have curled up and died; my hands would have frozen if a church full of people were sitting waiting for my music.

All my life I had tried to do what Martha had asked me – I had struggled to be as ordinary and as unobtrusive as possible. Deep in my heart I wanted to learn how to dance, but Martha didn't want me making a fool of myself in the ballet class that the class-one teachers ran in the gym on Wednesday afternoons. If I wanted to learn to dance I would just have to wait until I was eighteen, then I could learn with the dance teacher from the city, who came every winter to teach the village teenagers the foxtrot, the veleta and the English waltz. But I didn't do that either – by the time I was old enough to be admitted to the dance hall, no one went to his lessons. Things like the veleta had gone completely out of fashion.

Twenty-four

In the days when the Flemish widow had chased the joy out of the house, Camilla announced that she was going to get married. Caspar was going to Lourdes first and they would set a date as soon as he was back.

Martha nodded. She had given up trying to control her sisters' lives.

Caspar had been ill for some time. His hump was covered with sores and lumps that the nurses of the Home Nursing Service had been unable to heal. Ever since starting work at the brewery, he had been saving up to furnish his and Camilla's house in the style he most admired, that of the brewer – a man with expensive taste. Now Camilla insisted that the money could be better spent on a trip to Lourdes to seek a cure from the Holy Virgin.

Every year a hospital train bound for the South of France departed the city with hundreds of crippled and diseased passengers, all hoping to return healthy. Of all the people in the village who had gone to Lourdes, no one had ever come back healthy, and no miraculous stories had reached them from any of the surrounding villages either. Still, even though faith in the Church was faltering, everyone still had an unshaken belief in the Mother of God. Throughout the month of May, large groups of praying and singing pilgrims from all over the province headed for Roermond on their way to the Chapel of Our Lady in the Sand. There were processions to St Mary in Kevelaer, just over the border in Germany, and bus trips were organized to Belgium to worship Our Lady of Banneux.

Although he still believed, Caspar was reluctant to use the furniture money to get rid of his sores. But Camilla insisted. She told him that she would be just as happy with cheap furniture, second-hand if necessary – she could always reupholster it. She described their future furniture to Caspar in such glowing terms that even the brewer's interior paled by comparison.

On a Friday afternoon in May, Caspar left for the South of France in a train that reeked of disease. Camilla and I drove him to town in the van and he was plonked down in a wheelchair the moment he arrived. He had never sat in one before, but when he tried to get up to hobble over to the train, a nurse firmly pushed him back down. He hugged Camilla tight as if trying to leave a permanent impression of his body on hers. Camilla wasn't allowed onto the train and we couldn't see where they took him. The train started moving while we were still walking along the platform looking in the windows.

Long after he had left, we stood there waving at the train while tears flooded down Camilla's cheeks.

'I don't think he's going to get better,' Camilla said on the way home. 'Some people just weren't born for miracles.'

*

Caspar hadn't been born for miracles.

In a notebook he took to write everything down so that he wouldn't forget a thing when he was telling Camilla about it later, Caspar described how he was submerged every day in water that was so cold he could no longer bend his joints when he tried to go to Mass at the Grotto of Massabieille. He concluded each entry by wishing for recovery, but in the ink blots between the lines, you could read that he had long given up hope.

He died the day before the return journey. His coffin came back on the hospital train and was unloaded straight into a hearse. The city undertaker took him to the morgue. No one was allowed to see him – the body had already started to stink.

On Saturday afternoon he was buried. The church was full. On the coffin were two large wreaths, one from his sisters and one from the people in the street. There were no signs of life in the flower arrangements: nothing but gloomy greens and pallid flowers.

We were all in the church. Even Grandpa's widow and her son. She thought that her presence would lead to the neighbourhood accepting her – but the space next to her remained empty. Camilla still hadn't arrived when the time came for the priest to bless the coffin, which the pall-bearers had set down in front of the altar. Caspar's three sisters were sitting at the front.

Camilla was nowhere to be seen.

*

199

The priest was about to commence the Mass when a whisper shivered past the Gothic arches of the church. The congregation turned around. Camilla was standing in the doorway in a white dress, with white ribbons in her hair. Her bridal bouquet was a heart made of red flowers. Very slowly, she walked forward while the priest waited patiently for her to reach the front of the church, where she lay her heart on the coffin, half covering his sisters' wreath. Then she sank to her knees and stayed there.

The church stopped breathing while the eldest sister left her pew to take the floral heart from the coffin and lay it on the floor. Camilla stayed deathly still, and once the sister was back in her place, the organist struck up the opening notes of the Requiem.

The priest turned and began saying the Mass. He spoke compassionate words. The sisters sobbed loudly. Camilla stayed there on her knees. Her shoulders heaved now and then, but she didn't cry. After Mass she was the first to leave the church. Everyone let her go.

Moved by their sister's anguish, Martha and Christina cried as they followed Caspar's family in the funeral procession. Walking through the village to the cemetery, the sound of the church bells pursued us and turned the sunny Saturday into a day of sorrow. Passing the bakery, which was closed for once, I shivered.

Camilla did not join in the funeral procession.

She wasn't at the cemetery either, although for a moment I thought I caught sight of her behind a tree, close to Sebastian's grave.

Caspar was buried beside his father. Later we heard that before leaving for Lourdes he had bought a double grave so that Camilla could be laid beside him when she died. His sisters cheated them out of being joined in death.

We walked home in silence. We hadn't been invited to the family home for coffee and cake. That was an extraordinary slight. We should have joined in the grieving, if only as neighbours. They had even ordered the tarts from the new baker.

At the shop door, Martha hesitated and looked at us. 'Where's Camilla?' she asked, without expecting an answer.

'In her room probably,' said Christina.

We shuffled through the shop on our way to the house.

Never again will I forget Martha's cry. With a voice that was full of remorse and as cold as ice, she shrieked, 'Oh, no!'

Camilla was hanging from the banister in her white dress, the ribbons still in her hair.

She was buried on Wednesday afternoon, close to Sebastian and far from Caspar's grave.

Twenty-five

The shop had been closed since the Saturday of Caspar's funeral, and on the Thursday after we had buried Camilla, there was still no sign of anyone being ready to reopen the door. The journeyman baker dropped by each day to check on things, then went back to his boarding house to play cards with friends.

After breakfast my aunts just sat around staring into space. Until the widow seized the silence by its lapels.

'Who's going to do the shop?' she asked, looking from one to the other. 'I don't want anyone wearing black behind the counter, that's behind the times.'

The women in mourning looked from her to Martha, who just stared at the fat woman. The silence rustled like spilt salt.

Slowly Martha's cheeks reddened. Her mouth dried out and her pupils got tiny. Then she stood up and screamed, 'From now on, do it yourself! And you can bake the bread for all those windbags who never pay on time as well! I worked hard all those years to build up something, but I never knew I was doing it for a fat pig from Flanders! I didn't work for you, you dirty slob, and not for that . . . that drooling creep either! I did it for my sisters! And what do I get for it? I never had time for my own child, and the one I protected the most has killed herself. I'm broke and I hate God. I don't understand what He wants from me any more. Ask Him to look after you, I'm not going to. I've done enough. I've had it.'

She fell back onto her chair and burst into heavy sobbing. 'I did what I could. I did everything Mama wanted. I looked after you well, didn't I?' Her questioning eyes passed from one to the other. Christina stood up, laid her right hand on Martha's shoulder and squeezed gently. Martha breathed in deeply and continued, 'And now this bitch,' she pointed a trembling finger at the dumbfounded woman, 'comes here to take it all off us! I'll never forgive Father for this. I hope that wherever he is now, he can see what he's done to us. He always left all his dirty work to me. Without me, the business would never have got this big.' She glared at the widow, who returned her steely gaze with a look of astonishment and turned to the others for help. 'If you want the business, you can have it. I always hated it anyway. I can't tell you how many times I dreamed of never having to go into that lousy shop again . . . But you're going to pay us for our share. And right away. We worked hard enough for it,' she said, standing up so suddenly she knocked her chair over. She walked off, but turned in the doorway. Pointing at her 'half-brother' and with her voice breaking, she added, 'And I want to see this mongol's birth certificate because I don't believe that he's related to us.' Then she walked into the hall, slamming the kitchen door so hard that two panes shattered and glass flew all the way to the stove.

*

Her sisters didn't know what to do and started on all kinds of pointless chores like tidying up cupboards that weren't messy and washing clothes that only needed airing. But none of them went into the shop.

Late in the afternoon, Martha came back. 'We're going,' she said.

She went upstairs and started emptying wardrobes, piling the clothes up on sheets and tying the four corners to turn them into big bags. 'Anne? Vincentia? Who's driving? Bring the van around the front.'

Her sisters were too astonished to ask questions and too used to Martha's deciding things to raise objections. Without even knowing where they were going, they started packing their personal possessions into boxes and pillowcases. The van was loaded up until not even a mouse could have squeezed into the back. 'You come on bikes,' Martha said, after climbing into the front of the van next to Vincentia. She handed us the address.

That evening saw us all sitting at a battered round table in an old single-storey house that had belonged to a widow with ten married sons, whose rooms had been left untouched since their wedding days. The photos of football heroes and scantily clad starlets were still pinned to the walls. The sons had taken their mother to an old people's home because they had been unable to stop her from peeling enough potatoes for eleven people every day – now she could do it in the kitchen of the home. Almost all of the furniture had been left behind.

Marie, Anne and Christina made a second trip to pick up

their bridal chests, despite the protests of the Flemish widow, who claimed that they had no right to empty her house and threatened to call the police. That evening we used Christina's plain white crockery and the antique silverware the former mayor had given Anne when he went to the old people's home, where she still visited him occasionally. We drank two bottles of gin between us and everyone slept deeply and without dreaming.

Two days later the widow's lawyer appeared at the door with a young constable who didn't speak the local dialect. That made it hard for him, because when he tried to tell them that they had to return the delivery van that was parked in front of the house, the sisters refused to answer him in standard Dutch.

'I'm not driving an inch for that slob,' said Vincentia, hurling the keys at the police officer's feet.

The young policeman accused Martha of interfering with the course of justice and threatened to arrest her.

Marie picked up the keys and pressed them into his hands. 'Here, we're doing what you ask, aren't we? If fatso says it's hers, then it's up to her to come and drive it away. There's no law that says we have to play chauffeur for her. And don't forget, she doesn't have a driving licence, so she's not allowed to drive it, and if she does, you can arrest her, because that *is* against the law, and now piss off because we've got better things to do than listen to a brat like you.' And with that, she pushed him out the door and shut it behind him.

Everyone almost died laughing, and a little later the chief

constable appeared at their door and asked in the local dialect what was going on.

Martha showed him in and explained what had happened over a cup of coffee. The policeman, who had known the family for years, told them that they weren't obliged to return the car, but that they needed to realize that they weren't allowed to use it without the widow's permission.

And so the dark-blue Volkswagen stayed parked out the front until the rubber of the tyres dried and cracked and the van was sagging like an old man standing guard at the doorway of the sisters' new home.

From then on the widow sat at the till and the baker sold the bread, which he still baked faithfully every day – something the sisters resented deeply; they had expected greater loyalty.

They kept silent about the bakery. But they did need to discuss banalities such as financing their new household. They had no reserves – all their money was invested in the business – but needed bread and butter and potatoes and meat and vegetables, and suddenly they had to buy all kinds of things they had always taken directly from the shop.

Each of the sisters had a bank book that was beyond the reach of the slovenly widow. They used these to form a combined pot to pay for the first few weeks' rent, electricity, coal and food.

For the first time in her life, Marie made a financial contribution and emptied out her chests. She began using the cream-coloured crockery set and the silverware for special dinners. She piled her initialled towels up in the hall closet for general use, and her embroidered sheets were also used for the first time – after first being soaked in bleach for twelve hours to take the colour out of the embroidery: no one wanted to sleep between Marie's blood-drenched memories.

Marie and Anne got more and more jobs catering weddings, funerals and First Holy Communions. Vincentia got a job at the tree nursery with Clara, and I went to the domestic science school, despite Christina's protests. Martha and Christina stayed home. Neither of them had any experience of working under a boss and they were afraid that they wouldn't be able to adjust.

For want of anything better to do, Martha started turning the soil. Although badly neglected, the garden was still full of flowers and shrubs. The nurseryman supplied her with new rosebushes, which couldn't actually be planted out because it wasn't the right time. Oma told me to tell her that she had to do it at the new moon, but Martha just laughed – she was much too down-to-earth for 'that kind of nonsense' – and planted the seven rosebushes against the shed wall when it was full moon, just because that was when the nurseryman happened to deliver the plants. The bushes never blossomed and developed thorns as big as rosebuds.

Anne reserved a corner of the garden for the herbs she needed to add the finishing touch to her dishes, and the next-door neighbour gave us three chickens that had stopped laying and were already too tough to eat. Then, when the man from across the street gave us an old rooster as well, the hens suddenly became broody again, and supplied us with a couple of eggs every day – we had to search for them because we didn't have a coop. Like an elderly sheikh who is scared that someone is going to plunder his harem, the rooster pecked holes in our stockings if we so much as dared come near the hens.

One of the three hens had forgotten her laying routine, but received loving assistance from the elderly rooster: one morning he came into the kitchen with his comb up and poked around until he discovered the box with old newspapers. He then ran outside cackling, and returned soon after with the sluggish hen, which he pushed into the box. He hung around until she had laid her egg, then launched into a loud impersonation of clucking and kept it up until she began copying his strange gargling sound. From then on, he came into the kitchen with her every morning. If the door was shut, he pecked at the wood insistently until someone opened it to let in the hen.

One day the milkman presented us with a young pitch-black kitten. Then the farmer at the end of the street deposited an orphaned hedgehog on our kitchen table. The animal ran off every night – in the daytime Martha went looking for it and brought it back in the fold of her apron.

Our new life seemed to have completely replaced the previous one – it was as if the bakery had never even existed. I asked Martha how she had stood it for all those years.

'What else could I do?' she asked. 'I had three small children to look after and three sisters who had just left school. Was I supposed to take them to an orphanage? That's not how you treat your own sisters. And then, when they did their First Communion, in dresses Marie had embroidered that were far more beautiful than all the other girls' shop-bought dresses, then you feel so proud that you've managed, that you're grateful for having had the opportunity.' She was silent for a moment, then added, 'I don't know how I would have coped without them.'

'But how did you know how to run the shop? Did you always have enough money?' I asked.

'Of course not. You do what you can and you find ways to make ends meet. Different people help you with advice. Other things you find out by trial and error. Customers often gave me clothes. If they didn't fit, I had a seamstress alter them, often in exchange for a few tarts. Believe you me, if the water's up to your neck, you soon learn to swim.'

I had to laugh. Although Martha had learned a lot of things, she had never succeeded in conquering her fear of deep water.

Sometimes I went to town with Anne when she visited the former mayor. She explained her new life to him and told him about the people she and Marie cooked for, but he never listened to her words. The present was wasted on him. He had reverted to the days when they were together. Anne had never told me what had happened between them, but I could read their story in the tears in his eyes.

Vincentia too had never allowed her wounds to form a hard scab – she could never resist picking it open. She said that she lost all her memories the moment Martha showed her that men are cheats, but that was a lie. She knew exactly where they were, she just didn't dare to approach them, and when I touched upon them she became very quiet and then said, 'Yes, I still know everything about the days before I came here. I had lots of horses and I didn't need to tame them because they did exactly what I wanted them to. They were my friends and I was their friend, we shared the days and the nights, the sun, the moon and the stars – until the Indians came and started hunting us. After that I don't remember a thing, everything went black. I didn't see light again until I was walking over the heath with Sebastian: then I remembered the language of the horses . . .' She was silent for a long time and I forgot what else I wanted to ask her. 'Sebastian was like me,' said Vincentia. 'Later, when I saw Roy Rogers movies, I sometimes thought that he had gone to Hollywood, but that was nonsense of course. Sebastian looked a bit like him, he had small eyes like his and he had a good voice. But with us, everything was a lot more ordinary.' She laughed loudly and walked inside.

Christina was given a task that she had always longed for, but had thought impossible. We had been living for just two weeks in the house on the edge of the village, where there were no pavements and the grass grew alongside the raggedy-edged bitumen road, when two small boys appeared on our doorstep, dropped off like an anonymous box of Christmas presents. There was a knock on the door, and when Christina opened it, there they were, with one small suitcase between them, holding hands while a car raced off down the street. One of them was holding an envelope addressed to Clara. The enclosed letter was to the point: 'They're your brats. You look after them.'

The boys were identical twins and almost three years old, with big brown eyes and dark steely hair just like Clara's. They had Clara's cute button nose as well and smiles that begged for a hug.

Confronted with the children, Clara acted hurt. 'What am I supposed to do with them?' she shrugged. 'I never learned how to get on with kids.' She didn't say a word about where the children had been born – she was only just willing to admit to being their mother. She made no move to put them to bed, and since Christina had fed them, they cuddled up to her when they got sleepy, until she finally laid them in her double bed and took on the role of their mother.

She did that with dedication. She took them for walks through the marshes, where the swampy earth held tight to the skeletons of soldiers who never got a chance to go back to tell their sons about their acts of heroism. Their stories found their own way into the world, whispering in the bushes and burbling in the red water of the shallow streams. Aunt Christina knew the stories because she was able to listen to the wind and the water, and she kept them safe for when the boys were bigger.

I usually joined them for these walks. When I saw Christina's lost dreams taking her by the hand, I was frightened – I knew how hard and callous Clara could be. One day she would say that it was enough and that Christina should mind her own business. For now, Aunt Christina revelled in the unexpected motherhood that had come knocking on her door.

Twenty-six

Martha found a lawyer in the city who specialized in inheritance. It took him almost two months to establish whether the widow's marriage documents were genuine – they were, but her retarded son turned out to be the same age as Vincentia. He couldn't possibly be the sisters' half-brother, because Grandpa never went to Belgium in those days. The widow did have a right to a share of the inheritance, but the lawyer made up a statement for the amount of money that Martha had sunk into the business, including usurious interest and very stringent terms of repayment. He also calculated that the owner should have paid wages for all the years that the women had worked in the bakery. The largest sum of all consisted of taxes and social insurance that had never been paid, but would have been due if the sisters had received wages. The total was so high that the widow would need to sell the business immediately to pay her debts to her stepdaughters and the state.

The woman was used to blasting everyone away with her coarse voice, but when she saw the lawyer's figures typed out on an impressive number of pages, her face went whiter than the paper. Her voice abruptly lost its volume and became a mousy squeak.

She was so shocked by the arrogant attitude of this sly, slanty-eyed dwarf that she forgot that she could have challenged the bill – which was so exaggerated there wasn't a judge in the country who would have enforced it: most of the social insurance claims would have been proscribed by lapse of time alone – instead, she just pushed him out the door and closed the shop, even though it was only three o'clock in the afternoon.

She was gone the next day.

The shop remained shut and a week later Martha smashed the glass door to get in. The lawyer warned her that she would be in trouble again if her stepmother returned, but he immediately set to work fixing up her documents, which could never become fully legal – too many things were unclear. He invented debtors and buyers who had never existed and produced deeds of ownership that were as real as the new priest's teeth. But as long as there was no one to challenge her rights, there was no reason for anyone to doubt the validity of the documents.

The widow's disappearance presented Martha with a new dilemma. She was drawn back into the world of the bakery after having felt so free in the one-storey house, where she had even found time to talk to me and teach me to knit.

One day she said that it was a shame I couldn't sew properly. 'I always wanted to learn to sew,' she said. 'Imagine being able to do it as well as Camilla could. I don't understand why you don't like it. It's just wonderful to be able to turn a flat piece of fabric into a dress.'

Although I was unable to share her enthusiasm for dress-making, I did agree with her when she added that there was no longer much point in learning it. It was a dying profession. Everyone had become accustomed to buying their clothes off the rack.

She told me that Sebastian had taught her how to play the zither, but that she had never mastered it because she didn't practise enough. 'We never had time for things like that,' she said pensively.

One day she unexpectedly produced a small cardboard box with 'Höhner' printed on it. Inside was a mouth organ.

'This was with Sebastian's things,' she said. 'You can have it if you like. I have so little of his to give you. I can't even tell you what he was really like. I didn't know him long enough and I've remembered too many things I never wanted to see.'

My mother kept on putting off the decision about what to do with the bakery, and no one pressed her.

She had gone there to check on things with Marie and Christina. Before you had only ever seen cockroaches scurrying between the sacks of flour in the attic, but now they had descended to the oven and got stuck on the grimy baking trays. It had been so long since the linoleum in the shop had been washed that the dirt had set like cement. The glass in the display case had turned the colour of moss. It made Martha vomit, but the idea of returning made her feel nauseous as well.

To avoid thinking about it, they tidied the wardrobes. They found old trousers and pullovers that had belonged to the widow's son and bundled them up for the rag-and-bone man.

This could have been the start of a new life in a single-storey house on the edge of the village. A developer was interested in buying the building on the high street. He offered an amount that made Martha stutter when she repeated it to us. But she told us that we all had to decide together and, after studying thousands of different possibilities through a window that smelt of gin, a unanimous decision was made to return to the bakery.

But Martha had had enough of selling bread. Not only because the smell made her sick, but also because more and more people preferred the pre-packaged factory product that stayed fresh so much longer.

The bakery was renovated for Marie and Anne, who were now being asked to cater so many functions that their part-time activity had become a fully-fledged business. A gas stove with six burners was installed and the shelves were used to display the crockery, the serving dishes and the table linen, so that customers would know in advance what their festive dinner would look like.

Clara was the only one who didn't return. She married the nurseryman in a quiet ceremony and took the twins with her. When the boys started infant school Christina resumed their daily care – Clara lived too far outside the village to let the boys go to school by themselves. She took them to school in the morning and picked them up from our house late in the evening after they had been fed and washed. Her indifference infuriated Martha, but she kept her peace when she saw that the children softened Christina's bitterness about her life.

Since there were no longer enough staff to run the shop, the tasks needed reallocating. As usual, Martha took care of the most important matters herself without bothering her sisters, who were as satisfied as ever with this arrangement. A festive reopening of the shop was held to make sure that the customers were aware of the latest changes. Fitted out with new tyres, the van was now used for home delivery of groceries. Customers who wanted to use this service were given an order book and asked to pay COD. Most people, however, preferred to do their shopping in the modern shop and stood for hours at the till talking and exchanging gossip with the sisters, just like in the old days. Vincentia took the orders around late in the afternoon. Christina and Vincentia generally took turns at the till, while Martha provided customers with sliced cheese and ham and other products from the service section.

A city laundry now came to pick up the washing, and two unmarried sisters came in three times a week to scrub and mop the floors, wash the windows, do the dishes and generally take care of all the chores the sisters had done so reluctantly for so many years.

The new routine made time for things that had almost been forgotten. Vincentia remembered her old passion and went back to attending Sunday matinées at the cinema, which now showed German musicals. Anne resumed her day trips to the Eifel and the Ardennes. Martha bought a racing bike and went for relaxing rides to remote villages, often together with Christina and me. Only singing remained a thing of the past – at night we watched television.

I no longer saw the white women and Oma came less often as well. When I saw her, I asked about my father.

'Is he sorry that he just left me behind like that?'

'He did not just leave you behind like that. I have looked after you well. Just like I have looked after him when his father left him behind. Do not be ungrateful.'

She walked straight through the closed door and into the hall before I had a chance to ask her to explain.

One night I was lying in bed crying because I was scared that I would never find a husband and that no one would ever love me the way Sebastian would have if he had stayed. Suddenly I heard someone playing a mouth organ outside. Maybe the noise woke me up, or maybe it was just a dream. But I heard the music and walked over to the window. In the courtyard below I saw a man whose dark wavy hair fell in a lock over his forehead. He was wearing an Italian open-necked shirt, two-tone shoes and the wide trousers that were in fashion just after the war. Looking up at my window, he played a song that my aunts sometimes sang:

> Oh wild rose that blooms so free,
> Oh wild rose that's so lovely,
> I pluck this rose for you alone,
> Oh wild rose, my heart's your own.

He repeated it over and over, then waved at me, turned and walked away from the bakery, playing another melody:

Merry is a Gypsy's life,
Falala, falalee . . .

Epilogue

I was fifteen when the modern shop opened. I helped run it, of course. It went without saying and I didn't object, but it remained a decision Christina was unable to accept. She kept on bringing it up with Martha. It made me nervous knowing that she expected something from me that I couldn't do without hurting Martha. Things were fine just the way they were. My mother was proud of what she had built up, and by working in the shop I confirmed her sense of achievement.

I usually did the till. I wore a pale yellow smock with short sleeves – the aprons with crossed straps that my aunts had always worn had gone out of fashion. In the morning, before the shop opened, I helped fill the shelves, and after closing time I often had to mop the floor. That was a job I hated, and I did it holding my breath – that made it seem like I wasn't really there. I had already realized that dreams belong to the night, and that in the morning they withdraw to the hidden corners of your mind – which has more important things to worry about in the daytime.

It's a wonder I ever got married. More miraculous still, I found a man whose character was similar to my mother's.

He was an accountant at the sawmill, and had the kind of friendliness that has been scrubbed with laundry soap.

I've heard it said that children repeat the pattern of their parents, but I didn't search out a man who was as happy-go-lucky as my father. I found a husband who gave me the security Martha had never known. He let me do the things I had always wanted to do.

But when I started writing poetry, he said that poems were for lovesick teenagers and wondered whether he gave me enough love. Anxious not to hurt him, I gave it up.

When a musical I had written for my son's school concert was highly praised by the journalist from the regional daily, he pulled me down from the clouds by pointing out that the reporter was a friend of the headmaster's and was obliged to write a rave review.

My husband corrected me when necessary and encouraged me when I needed it. We had a good marriage.

I was less blessed when it came to motherhood. I didn't need to resort to certain devices to have less children than my grandmother. For a long time I didn't become pregnant at all.

That hurt terribly. I had imagined a family with as many voices as there had been in the bakery, and in my dreams I had added the voices of a father and a mother – as well as voices that weren't heard every day because they were the voices of aunts and uncles who only dropped by now and then. I had longed to listen to a choir that sang the song of a big family.

Fortunately we lived near my mother and were able to

celebrate holidays together. As my husband worked long hours and often had extra commitments in the evenings, I was free to work in the shop. Things were fine the way they were.

Finally I had my son, a beautiful child with steel-blue eyes and dark curly hair that tumbled down over his forehead when he was overdue for a haircut.

He was a difficult child. He demanded attention. He couldn't play by himself the way I had; he wanted me to join in and insisted on acting out strange stories in which I had to play the part of a dragon one minute and a princess the next. If I took him into a shop, he wasn't shy like I had been, but immediately struck up a conversation with the shop assistants about whatever happened to be on his mind. And never, not one single time, were we able to leave the shop until everyone had got involved with my child. And he was always being given something: a slice of sausage at the butcher's, an apple at the greengrocer's, a sweet at the chemist's. I invariably walked out of the shop embarrassed, with my son skipping along beside me.

At school he couldn't concentrate and was a trouble-maker. Despite this, we still sent him to high school.

My husband's nose and cheeks turned bright red when Christian opted for languages. 'Are you a girl, or what?' he said.

My son hardly ever did any homework. He saved his pocket money to buy a guitar and taught himself to play – my husband refused to let him have lessons unless his school results improved.

*

I loved my only child with all my heart, any mother would understand that, but we were light years apart. I feared that my son and I were repeating the pattern established by Martha and me, but there were differences I couldn't quite pin down. We fought out a conflict he could only lose, because he was younger and alone, and I had my husband's backing. We argued more and more often and his rebelliousness grew.

At sixteen he ran away. The police couldn't find him – a village police station doesn't have the resources to find a child who doesn't want to be found. I cried my throat raw and for months I could eat nothing but porridge. After a week my husband couldn't bear the sight of my tears and slapped me hard across the face – it was the first and only time. I looked at him and saw that he was relieved that the fighting was over and that he thought our lives would be good again as soon as I stopped crying.

I decided to stay with him, but the sorrow didn't leave me. Like nettles it grew everywhere, stinging your skin when you least expected.

Six joyless years followed and at times they swelled in my breast and overflowed into a black notebook I filled with poems. I sketched animals with sorrowful human faces. My life had become so ashen that even the flowers my husband bought me once a month were too scared to come out of their buds.

After six summers had passed without my noticing, I was suddenly left with nothing at all. My husband died.

Suddenly. From a rare disease whose name I still can't pronounce.

Two weeks later Aunt Christina died as well, the first of the sisters to die a natural death. At the funeral of my favourite aunt, I felt like I was walking through mist – the sky and the earth merged together and my horizons vanished. Far away I heard the foghorn of life passing me by.

Martha said that I should move in with her and her sisters. I needed time to think. The sisters had been living on the outskirts of the village for a few years. They had sold the bakery for a good price to a developer who wanted to build a new supermarket with flats above it (a modern innovation the village wasn't quite ready for – local council members successfully delayed planning approval).

It was a little over a year later, at All Saints. In accordance with the custom of the Catholic south, big white chrysanthemums were all over the cemetery, but I had made up red bouquets to lay on the graves of Camilla, Christina (beside her Jannes), Sebastian and my husband. I was standing by my husband's grave. Suddenly someone laid his hands on my shoulders. I could feel that it was a man: he was taller than I was, and he belonged with me.

I turned and hugged him. And I, who had been unable to shed a tear as a child, now cried like a baby, gasping for breath, and my own child held me tight with a warmth and compassion I had never felt before.

*

He went home with me, and for two days and two nights he told me about the last seven years. I could hardly remember them, but he had lived in distant lands I knew almost nothing about, places like North Africa and South America, where he had filled his time with valuable friendships that took the place of family.

He was now living in Spain, near Barcelona, but that was only recent. He was a musician: he made records and taught guitar. His first CD of his own compositions had been a reasonable success in Spain and he was working on a second. In spring he would be going on tour.

'Mama, why don't you come and live with me? There's nothing for you here. Your husband's dead . . .' – he didn't say Papa – 'and I saw that Grandma's shop is gone. Is Grandma dead?'

'No, Grandma's still alive. The four of them are still living together.'

'Then you don't need to feel guilty about leaving her alone.'

'But she's old. I can't go too far. What if something happened to her?'

'You can't sit around waiting till it does. At least come and stay with me for a while.'

'But Christian, how? Would I have to fly? I've never been on a plane.' It was true. My husband and I had never gone any farther than the Ardennes, and once to Brittany.

'There's always a first time,' my son laughed.

But I knew I wouldn't dare.

*

A week later he went back to Spain leaving an emptiness in my heart that was too big to fill with poems or sketches of animals.

After a thousand hours, I called him to say I was coming.

'Do you want me to come and get you?' he asked.

'No, I'll come by myself. I'm not going to have a crash the first time. Or am I?' I took a deep breath. My lungs sucked in the air with a voraciousness that surprised me and my heart pumped blood to organs that had been dead for so long.

Martha went to Our Lady of Perpetual Help to light candles for my hazardous undertaking. She was so nervous that she didn't dare see me off and left it to Vincentia to take me to the airport.

I got to know the child I had borne in my womb and had then tried to deform with the voices of my mother and my husband, and I saw that I had been leading Martha's life instead of my own. I had wanted so desperately to give her something, that I had lived out her need for security, and since I had given up everything for her, I had been unable to listen when my son tried to talk to me. Now we walked along the beach arm in arm and ate salted sardines. We drank gallons of Rioja. Christian taught me to dance. He sang songs for me, with tunes and lyrics I didn't know, except for one – unbeknown to me he had put one of my poems to music.

'I saw your notebook lying around and I thought the

poems were so beautiful that I wanted to use a couple on my new CD. You don't mind, do you?'

Of course, I tried to talk him out of it. I couldn't believe that they were any good. But he convinced me, and the beautiful melodies he composed to go with them brought tears to my eyes. We celebrated Christmas in the open air and on the beach we sang about shepherds watching flocks by night.

'You look so different,' said Martha when I showed her the photos. 'I hardly recognize you.'

I smiled and looked in the mirror.

I tried to make a story about the animals with faces by drawing new ones that weren't sad and writing captions to go with them. I started learning Spanish so that I could talk to my son's friends. I learned it faster than the rest of the class. In the end, I felt that the time had come to sell my house and began emptying wardrobes. I looked at the photos and paintings and books and knick-knacks, and asked them what they meant. I made signs saying CAN GO and KEEP, and laid them beside piles that kept on growing. I pulled apart the past like loose threads in a carpet until there was nothing but an empty space.

I picked up the telephone, called Christian and told him that I was ready to leave.

'You going to Grandma's? Or are you coming to live with me after all?' he asked.

'I'm not sure. First I want to travel.'

'Where?'

'I'm not sure. Actually, I am. I want to go to Mexico. You coming?'

'If you wait till the end of the tour.'

'Fine. As long as we're gone for my birthday. I don't want to give a party. I'm going to party with life itself.'

'You sound like a stranger, Mama.'

'Don't worry, come and get to know me,' I said and pulled open a bottle of Rioja to celebrate my decision.

When I opened the second bottle, someone said, 'Cheers, and pour us a drink as well.'

Oma and Christina were sitting on the oak sofa with the olive cushions.

'You drink too much,' Oma laughed.

'That's my business! I'm almost fifty, I've had enough of other people telling me what to do. I'm going travelling.'

'Are you going to write a book about the bakery as well?' asked Christina.

'Who knows? That's what you should have done, but I'm going to do all the things no one expects me to do.'

'That's my girl,' said Oma. 'Just like her father.' And she took a glass. 'Yuck, this is disgusting. Don't you have any gin?'

'Where have you been the whole time?' I asked. 'I was so alone.'

'We are always there,' said Oma.

'You just couldn't see us,' added Christina. 'The tears had covered your soul like so much moss.'

Once again, she had expressed it beautifully. I was moved and recharged my glass. 'Why don't I ever see Sebastian? There's so much I have to tell him.'

'You are still not getting it, are you?' said Oma. 'He is

closer than you think. It is now about time that you were learning to look with the heart.' And with that, she disappeared through the wall.

The new day wore a veil. I woke up on the floor and saw a red stain on the carpet and three empty bottles. My first impulse was to clean the carpet, but then I realized that the young people who would soon be living here would lay parquet floors anyway. Wool carpets were old-fashioned. This carpet could go!

Christian came to clear away the last few things.

'Hey, do you play the mouth organ? You've got so much stuff I don't know a thing about,' he said.

'It was your grandfather's,' I answered. 'You can have it. It's the only thing of his I have.'

He tapped the instrument on his palm and wet it with his lips before finally sucking out the melody that had been imprisoned inside it for years.

> Merry is a Gypsy's life,
> Falala, faa-laa-lee!

Astonished, I wondered where Christian had learned that song. People had stopped singing it before he was even born. He badly needed a haircut and his hair was hanging down in front of the eyes he had inherited from his grandfather. He took the mouth organ away from his lips and smiled. Stars twinkled in his voice.

Then I remembered what Oma had said. Had Sebastian

been given a second chance to show me how wonderful life can be? These things happen.

San Cristóbal de las Casas, Chiapas, Mexico 1998